This one is for
My sister Marjorie in Taos, New Mexico
My son Jamie in Dallas, Texas
My sons Scott and Adam in Washington, D.C.
And my wife and best friend, Fran, in Fort Pierce, Florida.

Also by Malcolm Mahr

FICTION

The Riyadh Conspiracy
The Secret Diary of Marco Polo
Murder at the Paradise Spa
The Mystery of DaVinci's Monna Vanna

NONFICTION

How to Win in the Yellow Pages
What Makes a Marriage Work
You're Retired Now. Relax.

The Orange Blossom Mob

Quiet men, like still waters,
are deep and dangerous.

~Portuguese proverb

PART I

…Prologue

BULLETS RICOCHETED around his chest like pinballs, fracturing ribs and puncturing FBI Agent Frank Fernandez' right lung. He was sent reeling backwards. Fernandez crumpled to the dingy, empty Miami warehouse floor. Warm blood poured down inside his shirt. The pain was excruciating, every breath a knife turning in the agent's upper body. He began to lose vision—a whiteout erased the emergency medical technician trying to save his life. Then the blackness swam up and over him in waves, and the SWAT team leader passed out.

Frank Fernandez commanded the special FBI unit in charge of a yearlong narcotics investigation involving multiple federal, state, and local law enforcement agencies. The Miami raid was intended to serve a warrant on Cesar Zúñiga, head of a notorious drug cartel. Zúñiga had forged the diverse cocaine warlords of Colombia into a single syndicate, succeeding the outfits of Cali and Medellin. The drug lord had made a rare visit to the U.S., and Fernandez had received a solid-gold insider tip. Zúñiga planned to personally supervise a major cocaine transaction worth multi-millions. Unfortunately, the Miami drug bust had come up empty.

Over the past decade, the FBI had experienced successes and failures. The successes often occurred in private—the failures appeared in full view of the media, which leveled a series of embarrassing charges against the bureau, including Robert Hanssen, the Waco standoff, the Ruby Ridge siege, Dmitry Sklyarov, Wen Ho Lee and Mir Aimal Kas. Ultimately, it would be the Miami fiasco that would prove to be the Bureau's most damaging failure—and would shake the FBI to its very roots.

APRIL THE TENTH marked Marcus Wolffe's sixty-fifth birthday; three days before, according to the FBI, he had ascended to *capo di tutti capi* of the notorious Gesumaria crime family. A muscular little man, five foot five, Wolffe had a slight paunch, by no means excessive for a man of his age. FBI analysts reviewing secretly recorded photographs reported the man to be plain-looking with a thin, lined, dark-complected face, indicating possible foreign birth. His nose and chin were fine and sharp. His dark eyes were steady and watchful under neatly trimmed dark hair.

Interviews conducted with Wolffe's neighbors revealed the man to be somewhat cold and detached, spare in speech, and polite. They defined Marcus Wolffe as a quiet man.

TWO WEEKS EARLIER, on a warm and breezy March morning in the Washington headquarters of the FBI, the executive assistant director (EAD) for urban crime, Richard Nurkiewicz, glanced at the front page of *The New York Times*. He felt blood pulsing behind both ears.

It's Not Just the Mafia Anymore

THE NEW YORK TIMES—"Today organized crime comes at us from every corner of the globe," reported FBI Director William Glenner. "We work to cripple these national and transnational syndicates with every capability and tool we've got: undercover operations, confidential sources, surveillance, intelligence analysis and sharing. We work closely with

Interpol and international partners to disrupt groups with global ties."

Director Glenner added, "I am planning to shift personnel from our Urban Crime Branch to our National Security Branch. We have achieved measurable progress in reducing the effectiveness of crime families. The New York Mafia has been expelled from its main bastions: private garbage carting, the garment center, the construction industry, waterfront cargo and their control of key unions. We are not folding up the program," the FBI head insisted. "We're constantly allocating resources where the perceived need is the greatest, namely counterterrorism and national security cases."

Richard Nurkiewicz was short and wide, mid-fifties, with a ruddy moon face. He had the body of a weight lifter and dressed in an off-the-rack J. C. Penney's dark suit. As he studied the *Times* interview, Nurkiewicz's brow pinched. Director Glenner had publicly announced plans to cut his department's staffing. He released a troubled sigh. "No fucking way, José."

MAFIA CRIME BOSS "FAT VINNIE" GESUMARIA gorged on steamed blue crabs in Colletti's Crab House, located in Essex, a blue-collar Baltimore suburb. Piles of claws and empty shells littered the beer-mottled, brown kraft paper table cover. Fat Vinnie was a rugged-looking man with a big stomach and large eggplant-colored circles under hard eyes; a tough Sicilian with a backbone of steel who believed it to be better to make money than war, but would kill in a heartbeat if necessary.

Gesumaria's bodyguards, the Santucci brothers, accompanied him everywhere. Small, dark-haired Tony Santucci had a thin, nasty mouth and lethal-looking black eyes. His brother Moose weighed close to three hundred pounds, a hairless, hulking presence with a huge chest, arms and shoulders.

With his meaty fingers, Fat Vinnie opened the reddish-orange shell of his jumbo crab, then snapped off the pincer claws. Greedily he scraped away the mustard and lungs, revealing luscious crabmeat. In his heavy tough-guy accent, Gesumaria grunted, "It don' get no better than this." Then he shoveled another large lump of spicy crabmeat into his mouth.

"Aaaaaawk! Aaaaaawk!"

Tony Santucci heard his boss gasping for air. He saw the big man's face flushed, contorted, clutching his throat, trying to cough, to breathe, to gulp for air.

"Vinnie's choking," Tony bellowed to his brother.

Three-hundred-pound Moose Santucci lumbered to his feet and wrapped his powerful, jiggling forearms around Gesumaria, jerking him off the ground. Vinnie thrashed and gurgled helplessly, eyes bulging while his giant bodyguard squeezed and squeezed until Gesumaria's breastbone crunched into his chest cavity, emptying all air from the lungs. The Mafia boss's head snapped forward like a car crash test dummy's. Arms, legs and torso went limp. He sprawled on the floor, twitching. Gesumaria fluttered one eyeball and flopped over dead.

"What da fuck?" Tony mumbled.

An arctic silence settled upon the restaurant. Mallet banging ceased. Crab house patrons sat in stunned silence. Word spread: "Mob hit." Waiters froze in place with lowered eyes. In minutes the restaurant emptied.

Tony knew the unwritten Mafia code. They would be held responsible for their boss's death. They were marked. "Come on," he yelled, pushing his confused brother into their late employer's Cadillac Escalade. Tony stomped on the gas pedal. "You'll like Canada, Moose."

STONE-FACED DETECTIVES QUESTIONED Colletti Crab House patrons and employees. Police stopped people at random along Eastern Avenue—people who might have witnessed the incident. The Baltimore detectives came up with blank stares, head-shakes and shrugs. Residents of Essex, Maryland were suddenly struck deaf and dumb and blind. A report of the death of Mafia crime boss "Fat Vinnie" Gesumaria flashed immediately to the head of the Urban Crime division of the FBI.

…3

MARCUS WOLFFE AND HIS WIFE ROSALIE lived frugally in a one-story house in a quiet, residential neighborhood in Pikesville, Maryland. When they married five years earlier, Wolffe had purchased the bungalow partly because of the tall Norway spruce trees and ten-foot ligustrum evergreen hedges that blocked the neighbors' view. Marcus Wolffe valued his privacy.

Rosalie had one extravagance: a masseuse named Vicki Vega. Vicki's mother had died from complications at childbirth. Her father, Charlie Colosimo, served as a Baltimore City councilman and *amico*, a close friend of the Gesumaria crime family. Vicki, in the sixth month of pregnancy, confided her impending motherhood anxieties to Rosalie.

"Vicki is expecting a baby—a boy," Rosalie explained to her husband. "She wants us to be the baby's godparents and attend the baptism and the luncheon in Little Italy."

The man stiffened and turned. Then he gave a thin smile. "A thoughtful gesture, but not a good idea."

"I'm bored, Marcus," Rosalie complained. "My life was not like this with Morris. He took me out to dinner, dancing and the theatre once in a while."

"Morris is dead. You know I don't like crowds. I agreed to move to Florida because you can't stand the cold weather, and you could be near your sister Gertrude and brother Bernie. After we settle in Fort Pierce, you'll develop new friends."

"I don't want to disappoint Vicki."

"Explain to her that we're Jewish. Catholic godparents make a profession of faith during the baptismal ceremony and assume guardianship over the kid. Besides, we'll be in Florida. Have Vicki check with her priest. He'll straighten her out."

6

When Rosalie raised the subject with her masseuse, Vicki answered, "Fuck that. I'll pick who I want." And so she did.

...4

NURKIEWICZ'S EYES WIDENED with excitement as he studied the Baltimore police report and the photographs of Fat Vinnie Gesumaria sprawled out dead on the crab house floor. He spread the pictures on the desk in front of him. The urban crime chief sat upright in his plush black leather chair, jacket off. His large corner office had Polaroid bulletproof windows that could not be seen out of—there was no view. The muted drone of a jet could be heard departing the Washington airport.

"If we play this one right, it will be a game-changer," he said to Agent Frank Fernandez, a tall, olive-complexioned man of medium height with thinning brown hair, wearing a wrinkled dark suit that looked as if he had slept in it. At fifty-one, Fernandez still looked lean and fit, but was the kind of man who would pass unnoticed. He regarded Nurkiewicz as smart, charmless and arrogant, a bureaucrat who used Mafioso scare tactics to bolster his career and his department's budget.

Nurkiewicz put down one photo and examined another. "I'll inform Director Glenner that Gesumaria's murder could set the stage for a major inter-crime family conflict. He can't cut my department if a crime war is threatened." Nurkiewicz rubbed his hands together, studying the photos. "Fill me in on the hit."

Fernandez opened his notebook and leafed through it. The odor of Nurkiewicz's drugstore aftershave lotion was giving him a headache. "The Baltimore police believe Gesumaria's bodyguards whacked him. Cause of death: *commotio cordis*."

"*Commo* what?" Nurkiewicz asked, drumming his fingers impatiently on his desk.

"*Commotio cordis*: A trauma to the chest wall. The forensic pathologist reported the victim suffered a fatal blow to the chest. The Santuccis probably used a steel crowbar or some other blunt object, and then the violent compression created a hydrostatic shock, driving blood back into Gesumaria's heart. Being obese, the guy's heart pounded harder than a normal person's, causing a lethal cardiac dysrhythmia."

Fernandez looked up from his notebook. "This case makes no sense. Why would 'made-men' kill their boss in a public place —in front of witnesses? They could have murdered him anywhere and disposed of the body. The Santucci brothers know the way things work—they're dead men. This is bullshit."

Nurkiewicz shook his head. He took out a monogrammed notebook. From an inside pocket came a gold fountain pen. "Here's the deal, Frank. I understand how the Mafia works. Killing Gesumaria in a public place is symbolic; shows the new boss has *cojones*. It's customary for the new don to show up within a few days of the hit. He will be introduced in a quiet sit-down to establish dominance, to let people know who's in charge. Crime families don't hold elections; it gives competitors a chance to organize support. Mafia strategy is changing; fewer celebrities like Hoffa and Gotti. The new bosses are tough and ruthless, like the old dons of the '40s. They keep low profiles.

"I want you to mount a full court press in Baltimore." He grinned wolfishly. "Under the new Domestic Investigations and Operations Guidelines, we can investigate anybody that attracts our attention, even without evidence of suspicious criminal behavior." Nurkiewicz pointed his gold fountain pen at Fernandez's chest. "I don't care how you do it—tap phones, eavesdrop, bribe snitches, search garbage. I don't give a shit. Just find out who this new godfather is. *Caprendo?*"

Fernandez emitted a sigh. "If I can locate a coming-out party, I'll need a surveillance vehicle with a laser parabolic, plus at least three agents."

"I'll order a van and a crew from the Baltimore office. And take Latisha."

"Who?"

Nurkiewicz pressed his silent intercom button. "Latisha."

A clear voice responded. "Mr. N, I'll brew coffee and fetch it, but don't expect me to serve it and wait on you. I do not perform menial tasks. I'm an administrative professional. You hear what I'm saying?"

"Latisha, come in please."

Fernandez raised an eyebrow. "New secretary?"

"Summer intern. Her name is Latisha Du Burns. Does that name ring a bell?"

"Congressman Joseph H. Du Burns' daughter?"

"The same—chairman of the House appropriations committee that monitors FBI appropriations. We need to keep the purse-string people happy. Otherwise I wouldn't have his kid here. She graduated law school, summa cum something, and couldn't find a decent paying job. Latisha thought a stretch with the Bureau would look nifty on her resume. Her father called Glenner, and presto, I have a new administrative professional or intern or whatever the fuck she calls herself. Between us, I think the girl is spying for her daddy, trying to catch us wasting the taxpayers' money. She gets on my nerves and makes the most god-awful coffee. Take her to Baltimore. Just keep her the hell out of harm's way."

"No thanks. Babysitting is not in my job description."

"Do it for my sake, Frank. I need to get that damn girl out of my office. She makes me nervous."

The door opened. Fernandez gaped at the tall, long-legged, black-haired beauty with almond-shaped eyes, flawless skin the color of polished teak, magnificent cheekbones, and a brashness that conveyed a confident sexuality. She stood composed, her arms folded. He sensed her eyes inspecting him, summing him up. Fernandez wondered what this dark beauty with those liquid emerald eyes saw. She made him feel uncomfortable.

"Latisha, I'd like you to meet Special Agent Frank Fernandez. You are being assigned to work with Frank on a very important surveillance mission." Nurkiewicz stood up. "That's it. You are both excused."

As they left, Fernandez asked, "How do you like interning with the FBI?"

"Hul-lo? Do you mean how do I like working deep in the bowels of the ugliest place in Washington? This Hoover Building looks like a huge damn tank ready to attack the Capitol. Should be torn down." She gave him a lascivious wink. "The Man's pushing me off on you, huh?"

Embarrassed, Fernandez didn't know what to say.

…5

HEAVY RAIN, HAIL AND DENSE FOG drifted off of the Chesapeake Bay, drenching I-95. Fernandez drove, squinting to be able to see the highway. Sitting next to him, Latisha DuBurns drummed her fingers, keeping time to music on her iPhone. After passing through the Baltimore Harbor Tunnel, she removed her ear buds. "Mr. N. thinks that I'm spying for my father."

"Are you?"

"Of course. We discuss everything. I love my father, but I can't live with the guy. He puts a damper on my social life. Daddy frets when I'm not home by midnight, and he's got the pull to activate the National Guard. I'm young. I got my whole life to deal with the problems that everyone has to face eventually: career, marriage, kids, money problems, infidelity and global warming, but I don't need to deal with all that stuff now. I'm not ready, understand?" Without waiting for a response she added, "So where are we going?"

"It has to do with the Mafia. We received a reliable tip of a 'goodfellas' sit-down. Nurkiewicz wants us to record everything. This heavy rain could pose a problem."

"Daddy says Nurkiewicz is not in Director Glenner's class —he's a loser."

"Are you pumping me for information about my boss?"

"Of course."

"Richard's father was a big kahuna in the Agency back in the '80s. He led a successful FBI operation, 'Devil's Dandruff,' which targeted cocaine distribution networks in Harlem, where there was the highest concentration of drug addicts in the country. Richard Senior's investigation resulted in hundreds of arrests, beaucoup people convicted and ten million in cocaine seized. As a result, at his retirement, Nurkiewicz' dad got the FBI's highest award, the Medal for Meritorious Achievement."

"I'm impressed."

Fernandez nodded. "When Richard, Jr. applied to the Bureau, they gave him a pass because of his father's reputation. But he's not the man his dad was. Being short, he sometimes acts impulsively. Without getting into a lot of Freudian stuff that I don't understand, he is probably trying to compete with his old man. Nurk has the ambition and ability to be FBI director. The genes are there, but the field experience isn't—nor is the character. He has an explosive temper. But I would never underestimate the guy. He is smart and crafty."

Fernandez found the exit ramp. Latisha could see Baltimore's bustling Inner Harbor through the mist. She sniffed the damp tang of the bay and the smell of the sugar factory across the inlet. The driving rain continued relentlessly. Traveling east on Pratt Street, they approached Little Italy. Frantic restaurant seekers in the century-old Italian neighborhood were hugging close to the row houses for shelter, veering outward only to avoid each other, their faces turned down out of the rain. The sky looked like gray steel.

Fernandez spotted the fog-enshrouded van parked across from the restaurant. "That's our mobile surveillance center." He pointed out the parabolic reflector dish mounted on the roof of the van. Fernandez pulled in next to a fire hydrant. With Latisha trailing behind, holding a folded newspaper over her head, he ran through the downpour. The rain drenched him before he reached the van. Three FBI agents huddled over their equipment. Fernandez recognized the crew leader, Charles Manion.

"Well, if it isn't Saint Fernandez," Manion snapped.

"Fuck you, Manion. You got a problem, take it to Nurk."

Manion eyeballed Latisha. "Why am I not surprised?"

Fernandez didn't bother answering. He introduced Latisha to the other two men in the crowded mobile surveillance center. She stared inquiringly at the nest of snaking black cables, laptops, flat-screen monitors, a generator, microphones and speakers. The seats had been moved flat against the wall, facing the equipment. It made for a tight fit.

The youngest agent, named Hooper, had close-cropped brown hair and unclouded blue eyes. "Excuse our electronic mess," he apologized. "This parabolic microphone is simply an ordinary microphone mounted inside a sound-reflecting dish that looks like a sideways U and can face in any direction. Sound waves hit the parabolic reflector, then they are channeled to our microphone and taping equipment."

"Awesome."

Hooper shrugged. The rain turned into hail, thumping noisily on the van's metal exterior. "Between us, the effectiveness of the parabolic microphone is exaggerated. They work well at distances of about 100 feet, providing the ambient noise level doesn't block out the targeted sound. In this rain, we will be lucky to get spit."

Manion turned to Fernandez and hissed, "You and I have unfinished business, *muchacho*."

A CORTEGE OF HEARSE-BLACK chauffeur-driven Cadillacs edged along the wet curbside of Massaro's Restaurant, a popular Baltimore La Cosa Nostra hangout. Large, broad-shouldered men laughed and pounded one another's backs. Their matronly-looking companions huddled under large umbrellas.

Inside the restaurant, guests were escorted to a private second floor dining area set up in a horseshoe-shaped table arrangement. Artificial red, white and green berry flower sprays and squat baskets of red Chiantis were neatly arranged on glossy white tablecloths. Drawn draperies blackened the picture windows facing onto High Street below. At the head of the horseshoe table sat the godparents, Marcus and Rosalie Wolffe.

Flanking the Wolffes were seated Vicki and Michael Vega, proud parents of the newly christened Joseph Charles Vega. To their left sat Vickie's father, Charlie Colosimo, the white-haired grandfather. His face was grave, and his pale gray eyes were chilly behind his glasses.

Colosimo tapped his wine glass for attention. "I welcome all of you here for this important occasion. Thank you for attending." Colosimo's voice boomed deep with a commanding bite. "Before we begin, it is appropriate to say *buon'anima* for our late and good friend, Vincent Gesumaria, rest his soul."

There were echoed mumbles from the assembled guests.

The host raised his glass. He pointed to the infant. "But life goes on. Thanks to little Joey. *Chindon*."

"*Salud a chindon*. Health for a hundred years," repeated the people in the room.

Colosimo chortled, emptied his wine glass and winked to the guests. "And now a word from our new godfather."

Marcus Wolffe appeared surprised that he was expected to speak. Nudged by his wife, he stood up slowly and spoke in a low, gravelly voice. People leaned in, straining to hear the words of the short, trim man with the dark olive eyes and deeply wrinkled brow. Wolffe cleared his throat and glanced at Rosalie. He opened his hands wide as if in apology. "There are times in life when your family's interest must be placed above your own." He shrugged. "And because of Little Joey, fate has decreed that this is to be one of those times."

Looking at the baby held lovingly in his mother's arms, Wolffe spoke directly to the child. "Be assured, that even though I will be moving my family to Florida, I will remain your godfather for as long as you wish for me to serve in that capacity."

"*Multo bravo*." The guests applauded vigorously.

'THAT'S A WRAP," Fernandez announced.

"Is the mission officially over?" Charlie Manion asked.

Fernandez nodded and stuck out a hand to shake. Suddenly, Manion crashed a haymaker of a right-hand punch into Fernandez' face, knocking him back against the van's wall. Pain filled his head. He tasted the blood spewing from his nose.

Latisha looked stunned, her hand to her mouth, eyes wide.

Manion smiled. "Pleasure seeing you again, Frank."

...6

"YOU LET THAT MAN GET AWAY WITH THAT!" Latisha scoffed.

"It's a long story," he mumbled.

Latisha slipped in her iPhone earbuds. She slumped in the passenger's seat, purposely ignoring him. The rain had slowed. Fernandez drove in silence, his right hand on the steering wheel, his left hand pressing the handkerchief trying to stanch the blood leaking from his nose. Fernandez exited the Baltimore Washington Parkway at West Nursery Road, made a turn into Hammonds Ferry Road, and parked. He put on the parking brake, turned off the engine, and looked at Latisha. "Do you like crab cakes?"

"WHAT?"

"Crab cakes. Do you like crab cakes?"

"What I'd like is a bathroom." She got out of the car without speaking.

Seated in the dimly lit, wood-paneled bar area, Fernandez ordered two crab cake platters, broiled not fried. "Cole slaw?" asked the waitress, a short brunette with a heart-shaped face. "And ice for your nose?"

"Yes and yes."

When Latisha returned, they sat in a stiff silence. She stared at his nose covered with dried blood. "Why did that man call you a saint?"

Fernandez took a long drink of ice tea. He put his palms together in front of his lips. "I did something that embarrassed my colleagues. In the good-old-boy FBI network of ex-jocks and frat boys, loyalty trumps truth."

Latisha raised her eyebrows.

"In 1993, the BATF—"

"Who?"

"The Bureau of Alcohol, Tobacco and Firearms. They mishandled a raid on a dissident religious community near Waco, Texas. Maybe you read about it. This guy, David Koresh, claimed to be God and threatened an apocalypse if federal agents stormed the compound where his followers were encircled. The FBI and the Army were called in, and they mounted a fifty-one day siege. It ended tragically. According to official FBI documents, the Branch Davidians ignited a suicidal pyre. In the inferno, 74 men, women and children died—including twelve kids under five years old."

Latisha shuddered involuntarily.

"Four years ago, I was in the FBI's hostage rescue team warehouse in Quantico looking for equipment. In a corner I spotted four dusty corrugated boxes with no markings. Out of curiosity, I opened the top box and found tapes and documents relating to the 1993 Waco incident. It surprised me, because FBI officials had sworn in court that such evidence did not exist.

"The first document I read reported that starting at dawn on April 19th, Army tanks rammed holes in the main Branch Davidian building and pumped CS gas into the structure. CS gas is a tear gas, sometimes used as a riot control agent." Fernandez pushed back his half-eaten plate. "The buildings became saturated with in-flammable CS gas and spilled kerosene. Around midday, two military pyrotechnic devices were fired into the main building. I believe that those flash-producing projectiles sparked the fire that spread through the complex of buildings and—" He paused. "For some unexplained reason, Waco fire department trucks were prevented by the FBI from approaching the inferno. To make matters worse, after the fire, the burned-out ruin was razed in an attempt to remove all evidence."

"What did you do?"

"I telephoned the FBI director. Bill Glenner and I go back a long way. Glenner dispatched a team to seal and take possession of the four boxes. He contacted the attorney general. She called a press conference and conceded that after six years of denials, pyrotechnic tear gas canisters had, in fact, been used at the Branch Davidian compound in the assault that ended with the deaths of some 80 Davidians. The attorney general implied that the FBI had misled her. The public exposure caused embarrassment and ruffled feelings throughout the Bureau. Somehow, I was named as the whistle blower, the virtuous, but disloyal team player, ergo: Saint Fernandez."

Latisha emptied her plate and folded her napkin. "Now, are you going to tell me why that guy slugged you?"

"I slept with Charlie's wife."

…7

"IT RAINED," Fernandez explained to Nurliewicz. "It rained *hard*. With the heavy squalls and the low decibel level in the restaurant, it made eavesdropping sporadic. We could only get fragmented sound bites on tape."

Nurkiewicz shot a curious glance at Fernandez' face. The hit on the nose lingered as a bruise. "Who's the new Mafia boss?"

"Name is Wolffe. Marcus Wolffe. A waiter pointed him out. We snapped this photo as he left the restaurant."

"Wolffe; a Jewish name. Unusual. Hasn't been a Jew Mafioso since Lansky. Let me see the photos." He grunted noncommittally. "These pictures are for shit."

"Hard to take good photos in a downpour. Photograph 34-10-B is grainy, but I think you can make it out."

Nurkiewicz squinted. "Short and wiry, like Lansky. Think he could be related?"

"Bit of a stretch." Fernandez handed his superior two typewritten pages. "Here's the transcript. A man named Colosimo, a friend of 'Fat Vinnie,' arranged the party. They were goombahs."

From the transcript, Nurkiewicz read aloud, " 'There are times in life when your family's interest must be placed above your own. And because of Little Joey, fate has decreed that this is to be one of those times. Be assured that even though I will be moving my family to Florida, I will remain your godfather for as long as you wish for me to serve in that capacity."

Nurkiewicz grumbled, "You got to give the bastard credit, he told it like it was."

"I don't understand."

" 'Little Joe' means 'mob hit' in Mafia lingo."

Fernandez watched angry flares of red explode high on Nurkiewicz's cheeks. "Wolffe is moving to Florida. Talk about balls.

In one stroke, he nails Gesumaria's territory, then plans a takeover in Florida, probably from Palmisano's Tampa mob.

"Have Latisha order a complete background check. I want Wolffe's state and federal records on my desk by morning. Have them e-mailed or faxed from wherever they are stored. I want to know Marcus Wolffe; where he lives, how he lives, home and cell phones, everything. Don't forget tax data, credit cards, Social Security, school records and military service. A person leaves tracks like a grub worm —we all do."

As an afterthought, Nurkiewicz added, "And have Latisha check out Lansky's family. Maybe this guy *is* related. I'll talk to the director. This is no time to cut staffing. If Wolffe carries out his plan, he will be the most powerful organized crime figure in the country since Meyer Lansky—the godfather of the godfathers."

"Aren't you overreacting a little?"

"Listen to me, goddamnit. If you don't obey my orders, mister, I'll find someone who will. Then you can go back to picking lettuce—like the rest of *your* kind."

Fernandez stared dumbstruck. He knew Nurkiewicz had an explosive temper, but the ethnic family slur was intentionally nasty, delivered by a smart, cagey operator who resented Fernandez' relationship with the director. A heated verbal or physical response could result in his transfer or even termination. Fernandez clenched his teeth, swallowed his pride and remained silent. Inside he steamed.

Budget Cuts Target Police Force

SCRIPPS TREASURE COAST NEWSPAPERS--
Fort Pierce Mayor Willie Westlake has announced
that with the recession affecting governmental budgets
at every level, the city has had to cut police staffing.

"The public needs to realize we don't have a
magic wand, and Fort Pierce does not have the necessary resources in these tough economic times.
We're not going to have deficit spending, and we're
not going to borrow from future generations, so we
will make do with fewer police officers on the
streets."

Before becoming Fort Pierce mayor, Westlake served as a consultant to the Pentagon. He explained, "We dealt with budget problems by outsourcing policing activities to private agencies. It
worked in Kabul; it will work in Fort Pierce. The
mayor's outsourcing program is called 'Partners on
Patrol.' According to Westlake's POP Rules of En-
gagement, task force members will be instructed to
use only the minimum force, consistent with the accomplishment of his or her mission."

...9

ALL FIVE MEN HAD THE WORN LOOK of Florida re-
tirees. They hunched around the table drinking steaming black coffee, telling stale jokes, reminiscing about the old days and growing
morose when the subject got around to their own ailments. The old
Mafiosos had had their brushes with the law and survived.

"My wife's giving me a headache," griped "Fast Eddie"
Rizzo, a short and bony man in his seventies. After serving five
years in prison in New York State, Edward Rizzo had received a
parole and moved to Florida. "Dolly wants me to take over her
dead brother's business; a locksmith barely scratching out a living
installing alarm systems and operating out of the back of his van."

"Whaddaya got to lose?" Mike De Luca said. "In the summer it's hot as hell and the goddamn no-see-ums will kill you."
The broad-shouldered, big-boned, square-jawed man added, "It's
cash business, plus you get to drive around in an air-conditioned
van, and the widows who call you will be lonely and appreciative."

"And horny," Sal Scarlotti chipped in. Scarlotti was frail-
looking with thick glasses, about 145 pounds, neatly combed white
hair, and a pencil-thin mustache that looked pasted on.

"Locksmithin's down your alley, Eddie," remarked "Bats"
Battaglia, a tall, gaunt man with a wrinkled, hard face. "Ain't no
safes nor no locks you can't handle."

The fifth member of the group, "Bernie the Attorney" Rothstein, looked up from his newspaper. Attorney Rothstein was
paunchy; he wore a tailored gray suit, red bow tie, and perfectly fit-
ting dentures, and his hair was dyed a dull brown that didn't match
his white eyebrows. He had a sharp nose, and his eyes were partly
hooded. "Edward, did you say your deceased brother-in-law owned
a security services company?"

"Yeah. The Orange Blossom Security Agency."

Rothstein chuckled, folding the paper. "Our budget-conscious mayor is supplementing the police with private security companies. You guys are bored and worried about the government screwing around with your Social Security and Medicare. Edward's brother-in-law's company is eligible be an arm of the Fort Pierce Police, and we would get paid for it. Not a lot, but it's a start." Rothstein quoted from the newspaper, " 'According to Mayor Westlake, task force members will be permitted to use minimum force, consistent with the accomplishment of his or her mission.' "

"What's 'minimum force,' Bernie?" Bats Battaglia asked.

"I believe broken kneecaps could be legally construed as using 'minimum force,' Joseph."

...10

FERNANDEZ AVOIDED LOOKING directly at Nurkie-
wicz. He was still feeling rankled. "Marcus Wolffe's family member in Florida is his brother-in-law, Bernard Rothstein," Fernandez
reported. "Latisha dug the information from their phone records."

"You can't be serious?" Nurkiewicz's features hardened.
" 'Bernie-the-Attorney' Rothstein served as house counsel for the
mob. He must be in his eighties. Jimmy Hoffa hired the guy to get
him off union corruption charges. Then Rothstein arranged kick-
backs of millions to Hoffa from the Teamsters' pension fund. He
got disbarred, but was never indicted."

Nurkiewicz inhaled deeply. "If Bernie the Attorney is
Wolffe's *consigliore*, it's serious shit. Advise the Fort Pierce office
to initiate round-the-clock surveillance on Rothstein and Wolffe.
Have them find out everywhere they go and photograph who they
meet with. And I want a phone tap on Wolffe's new house."

"I'm on it," Fernandez said, without emotion.

Nurkiewicz' face crinkled into well-honed exasperation. He
pressed the intercom. "Latisha, where is the background check?"

"Coming, Mr. N. Got to wait 'til my nails dry."

Nurkiewicz opened a red file folder containing Marcus
Wolffe's certificate of service form 217A. "Honorably discharged,
and he received the Vietnam Service Award," he groused. "His
MOS listed as 25M. What's that?"

"I checked with the Pentagon," Latisha said. "Sergeant Marcus Wolffe served as a multimedia illustrator responsible for producing visual displays and documents."

Nurkiewicz pressed his hands against his temple and sighed.
"What else?"

"The man has been married for five years; wife's name is
Rosalie. Her first husband died of a heart attack in 2000. They

have no children. Wolffe's age is listed as sixty-five." She shrugged. "When I saw the man leave that restaurant in Baltimore, he looked older than sixty-five. Might have been the rain and all."

"Did you have his tax records checked?"

"Nothing irregular. Wolffe withdrew an average of forty thousand a year from his IRA account, and now he's eligible for Social Security. His wife Rosalie has money from the first husband's insurance. I also reviewed the Crime Information Center's database. Wolffe is squeaky-clean, never even a parking ticket. His medical records will be in tomorrow."

"Where was he born?"

"Homestead, Florida is listed on his discharge papers. No birth certificate on file."

Nurkiewicz gave her a hard look. "How come?"

"According to the Florida Department of Health, in 1992, a Category 5 hurricane named Andrew struck Homestead a direct hit. It destroyed the courthouse and all records."

"What about computer backups?"

Latisha shook her head. "Back then Homestead was a small town; no backups."

"HERE'S THE MEYER LANSKY INFORMATION." Fernandez entered, holding black coffee in a Styrofoam cup in one hand and his notebook in the other. "Meyer Lansky's real name was Maier Suchowlansky, born in Poland in 1903, died in Miami January 14th, 1983. It's hard to find dots connecting the two men, other than their short stature and dark complexions, and both hung out at libraries. Lansky had three dysfunctional kids: one, Buddy, a quadriplegic; a daughter, Saundra; and Paul, a West Point graduate who deserted his family and became emotionally incapacitated."

Nurkiewicz drew a deep breath. "Wolffe's birth records mysteriously disappeared. Maybe he's Lansky's bastard son."

26

Latisha penciled in some figures. "Theoretically, it's possible. If Wolffe is sixty-five, he was born in 1947. Mr. Lansky would have been forty-four."

Fernandez shook his head. "There's no way Lansky and Wolffe are related."

"Listen to me for once, Frank," Nurkiewicz stated coldly. "Lansky dealt in stolen cars, drugs, shylocking, pornography and murder. If there is any blood connection between Marcus Wolffe and Meyer Lansky—any conspiracy brewing that could bite us in the ass—it's important that we get to the bottom of it. Omertà may be dead; the Mafia isn't. And please try to remember that I am the one in charge of this department. The last mission you were in charge of didn't fare well. Did it?"

Fernandez felt his face grow hot. He shot back angrily, "The Bureau has more important things to do than cooking up Mafia conspiracy theories just to expand your fiefdom. Here's another conspiracy theory you might want to check out, Richie. Word on the street has it that Albert Einstein was killed by the Mafia—because he knew too much."

Latisha stifled a laugh, biting her lip so that her giggles wouldn't be heard. Nurkiewicz noticed. He worried that the bitch would report the incident to her father. He raised both hands in a peaceful gesture. "Maybe I deserved that, Frank. Glad that you got it off your chest. Meeting adjourned."

After they left, Nurkiewicz glanced at his father's picture on the wall. He grit his teeth, angrily kicked over his trash basket, then slammed Marcus Wolffe's red file folder down on his desk—the papers strewed everywhere. Nobody ever talked to him that way and got away with it.

...11

THE LARGE AMERICAN FLAG sat atop the flagpole at the Fort Pierce Police Station. The Florida flag with its red diagonal stripes and state seal fluttered in the center position, with the smaller Fort Pierce flag at the bottom. At 9 o'clock, a 2006 Ford E250 van parked in the station lot. "Orange Blossom Security Agency" was spelled out in bold letters on both sides of the vehicle.

Salvadore Scarlotti stared at the long, low, one-story brown brick structure. A forest of tall radio masts appeared bolted to the roof. "This is an occasion," he told "Big Mike" De Luca. "First time you ever been in a lockup with no cuffs on."

Joseph Battaglia leaned heavily on his cane as he limped toward the entrance. Eddie Rizzo locked the van and joined the group as they entered the neatly appointed lobby with glass cases of trophies displayed against the wood paneled walls.

"Can I help you... gentlemen?" asked the receptionist.

"We're here for the orientation."

"Partners on Patrol?"

"You got it, sweetheart." Fast Eddie winked.

She raised her eyebrows and stifled a laugh that dissolved into a fit of coughing. She pointed silently to a door across the lobby. Inside, Bernie the Attorney sat alone at a conference table, reading the paper. Rothstein signaled two thumbs up.

A large African American woman with peppery white hair entered the room. She looked to be at the tail end of her forties and on the heavy side. She nodded absently to the group as she moved to the podium to arrange her papers.

"I am Sergeant Vesta Jones," she announced, looking down the conference table, pausing and taking a deep breath. "Who the hell are you guys? Did you escape from some nursing home?" She picked up her papers, preparing to leave.

28

Rothstein unlaced his fingers and leaned forward. "A moment, if you please, Sergeant. My name is Bernard Rothstein. I represent the Orange Blossom Security Agency. The City of Fort Pierce does not wish to invite an age-discrimination grievance suit, do they? I can verify that these civic-minded gentlemen all have special skills and previous experience in maintaining order in communities up north. Like myself, they are voters determined to see that the Fort Pierce Police force is returned to its normal staffing complement at the earliest possible moment. Until then, they are eager to volunteer to serve their community."

Vesta Jones emitted a loud groan. The middle-aged, firm-breasted sergeant was wide of hip, with dark, rich skin. She spoke slowly, deliberately. "Mr. Lawyer, your clients will have to sign waivers. Fort Pierce can't be held responsible for—"

Rothstein held up his hands. "Not a problem. They are covered by both Medicare and a generous company health plan."

"Fuck's he talking about?" Rizzo whispered to Scarlotti.

Sergeant Jones said, "Unfortunately, our city of Fort Pierce consistently ranks as one of the more violent cities, not only in Florida, but in the whole damn country. Since the latest budget cuts, we are now down thirty-two positions. As a result of dismantling our police force and the terrible economy, crime is on the increase."

"Can you share with us your biggest problem areas?" Rothstein asked.

"We recorded five hundred violent crimes last year," Jones announced. She glanced at her papers. "Ten homicides, 25 rapes, 135 robberies and 330 aggravated assaults. Non-violent crimes were over 2000, mainly burglary, larceny and theft."

"What part do drugs play, Sergeant?"

"Connected at the hip," she answered with a slow tilt of her head. "What's most scary is the rise of prescription drug abuse. Ten years ago prescription drugs caused ten percent of crimes. Today, it is more like fifty percent."

"No shit," Scarlotti exclaimed. Jones glared, shook her head, took another deep breath and continued. "If someone has an injury, they go to their doctor and get a prescription for Oxycodone or Oxycontin. They get addicted. Then they want more. Empty their bank account. Sell valuables until they hit rock bottom, then start stealing to support their habit."

"Where do they get the stuff?" Eddie Rizzo asked.

"Kids don't smoke pot like they used to. They go to Grandma's medicine cabinet. And we got pushers for all kinds of drugs operating out of houses or schools. The worst are on street corners. Once in a while we run some cars through there and run a bust. And it doesn't do a goddamn thing. You can bust these kids, see, and you can bust the users, but so what? The kids serve no time on the first couple of arrests, especially if there is no big quantity to speak of. The users get a night in jail, if that much, and do community service. And the kingpins go untouched."

Rizzo persisted. "How do they operate?"

"First, you got the steerers who lead the customers to the pitchers, who make the hand-to-hand transactions. And then there are the lookouts, and the moneymen who handle the cash. The ones just into the business, always the youngest, they're the ones who touch the heroin, the rock, the cocaine and prescripts. And even they don't carry it on them. You look real close, you see they're always nearby a place where they can hide a crack vial or a dime in a magnetic key case. But you don't want to be messing with those people, hear?" She glanced at her watch. "Here's how 'Partners on Patrol' works.

"Effective immediately, you... men are officially special deputy police officers participating in the POP Task Force. You will operate your vehicles with POP magnetic signage on the sides for high visibility enforcement. What we want is a *presence* on the streets—not interaction. You will not, I repeat *not* respond to any emergency calls you hear on the police radio."

Jones picked up a sheet. "Under GO-RAR-901.07, entitled 'Use of Force,' " she said, not quite smiling, "it provides that you are allowed to use only the minimum amount of force. Understand? We don't want you involved in anything that could cause you to end up in a nursing home. Operate in teams of two. Rotate nighttime hours —if you can stay up that late. Remain in your vehicle at *all* times. You are our extra eyes on the street. We will meet here at the same time next week."

She looked at Rothstein. "Tell your boys to turn in weekly gas expenditure chits for reimbursement. We also pay a per diem of fifty dollars each."

Rothstein raised his bushy white eyebrows and fingered his glasses. "Sergeant Jones," he intoned quietly. "Now that the meeting is officially over, may I ask you a question—off the record?"

"Depends on the question."

"If you had a wish list, what we used to call a 'Get Out of Jail Free' pass, and you could do *whatever* you wanted to cut down on crime in Fort Pierce, without any fear of recrimination—whatsoever. What would you do?"

Vesta Jones gave Rothstein a hard stare. "No tape recorders in the room?" Rothstein nodded, raising his right hand in a Boy Scout salute.

The sergeant raised her eyebrows and grinned. "You never got this from me. Hear? First, I would go after the dirty doctor—all he wants to do is make money. He opened a pain clinic on Ocala Avenue this year and sees as many people as he can, prescribing Oxycontin to anybody with a hangnail."

Jones shrugged and lifted a second finger. "Drive-by shootings are on the rise. We know who's doing it. Guys wearin' flay baseball hats, FUBU pants, pumped up bass music in their Lexus cars with those spinner rims and FDS low-profile tires.

"Number three," she clicked off, "the state attorney's office gets hundreds of domestic violence calls reporting guys who beat on their wives. And then there are the 194 registered sex offenders in Fort Pierce. Everybody knows who these people are. The list is on Google." She smiled. "Five cents' worth of lead would cure the problem."

De Luca cupped his hand to his ear and whispered to Rizzo, "What she say?"

"Shoot the fuckers."

"Thank you, Sergeant," Bernie Rothstein said. He added, "Any final wishes?"

She inhaled deeply and nodded. "I would particularly wish to be able to interrupt the street level sales of heroin and cocaine on the corner of North 23rd Street at G, especially Friday and Saturday nights."

Clear anxiety crept into her voice. "If any of this ever gets out, I'll be a greeter at WalMart this Christmas."

Deadly Year for Domestic Violence

TREASURE COAST NEWSPAPERS—According to Marjorie DeCosta, president of the Fort Pierce advocacy group *Empowerers*, "It has been a pretty deadly year around here. Crimes reported as domestic violence-related ranged from stalking and threats to assault and murder. Increased unemployment in the current economic doldrums may be spurring more battering, but not necessarily because of financial pressure on couples," DeCosta added.

"Domestic violence is about power and control, not necessarily anger and stress," she said. "With more people out of jobs, couples are forced to spend more time together at home, which creates more opportunity for trouble."

While official figures don't yet confirm a relationship between tough times and domestic abuse, it has shown up in other areas. Burglaries and theft are up just about everywhere on the Treasure Coast.

...13

"YOU GOT A GOOD DEAL FOR TWO-FIFTY," Bernard Rothstein confided to his sister. "Three years ago these oceanfront units were going for five hundred thousand. If the economy ever picks up, this apartment will double in value."

"I guess," Rosalie responded with feigned enthusiasm.

"And it's safe," he added. "Ocean Village is a gated community. Where's Marcus?"

"He takes long walks on the beach. *Alone.*"

"Are you two having a problem?"

"Bernie, you know me. I'm a people person. This place has water aerobics, Pilates, Zumba, writer's group and stuff like that. But I got remarried so we would be able to do things together, you know? Morris took me dancing, movies— "

"Face it, Rose. Morris is gone, and Marcus is different. Seems like a decent guy, maybe a little on the quiet side. How long you been married now?"

"Five years." She inhaled deeply. A tear crept into the corner of her eye. "I don't think I know the man. He moves so quietly that sometimes I don't hear him come into a room." She looked anxiously towards the front door. "And he is always watching."

"Watching what?"

"Everything. Sometimes he doesn't say anything, just sits watching people on the beach. And the man talks in his sleep—"

"Who doesn't?"

"But he speaks in different foreign languages."

"That's not surprising. He served in Army Intelligence. You're a Piscean, Rose. Don't start imagining things."

She blushed. "And he has scars all over his body."

"For Christ sakes, woman, your husband nearly got himself killed in a plane crash. What do you expect? You need to keep busy, and I've got just the ticket."

Rosalie smiled thinly. "Tell me."

"The U.S. Attorney's Office on Second Street needs volunteers to man their domestic violence hotline. Leave it to Bernie. I'll get you in. Don't worry."

Rothstein stood up to leave. He glanced at the silver-framed wedding photograph of his sister and Marcus Wolffe on the sideboard. Removing his iPhone, he snapped a picture. Outside in his car, Rothstein e-mailed the photograph with an attached message.

RothsteinLaw to CarmineD
3:35 PM
April 20
Carmine: Need a favor.
Check out guy in photo. ASAP
Bernie

CarmineD to RothsteinLaw
3:40 PM
April 20
Bernie: Looks like he's had work done.
If it's who I think it is.
You don't want to know!
Carmine

...14

AT THE STATE ATTORNEY'S OFFICE, Rosalie reported to the spousal abuse section. It had been recently renamed the Domestic Violence Call Center. Her telephone hotline duties were explained and clearly outlined in written instructions.

When a call comes in, the victim-abuse operator is to record accurately the information. At all times the operator is to project to the caller a calm, objective demeanor, and above all, express no emotion or opinion as to the merits of the alleged victim's claims. Then immediately direct the Call Report to the appropriate authority, the officer on duty.

On Rosalie's second night of duty, a distress call came in on her hotline.

CALLER: "My name's Joyce. I've got a problem!"

ROSALIE: "Go ahead."

CALLER: "My husband is drunk. He's slapping me around."

ROSALIE: "Where are you, dear?"

CALLER: "Locked in my bedroom. He's pounding on the door. Help me."

ROSALIE: "OK. OK. Settle down. Give me your address."

Rosalie rushed to the outer office, where a large, heavyset police officer with a huge round face sat reading *Playboy Magazine*.

"Hurry, please," Rosalie urged, handing him the victim's address. "This woman is being threatened by her husband. She's afraid he will hurt her."

He gave her a knowing smile. "You most be new," the duty officer groused. "Most of the calls we get are a waste of time. Half

36

the women are drunk or pissed off for some reason. When the patrol car arrives, everything is usually lovey-dovey. Besides, with the new reduced staffing, we need our patrols to prioritize their time and keep a close eye on the gang activity around Lincoln Park and the high crime areas. Sorry, lady."

Rosalie returned to her post. The call button lit up.

CALLER: "Are you sending help?"

ROSALIE: "Is this really an emergency?"

CALLER: "Oh God! Oh God. Can't you hear—he's kicking in the door!"

ROSALIE: "Joyce, try to stay calm."

CALLER: "Stay calm. Goddammit, I'm gonna die. Oh Jesus!"

Rosalie took a deep breath, then whispered so the police officer wouldn't hear, "Don't worry, honey, we'll fix that son-of-a-bitch." She dialed Rothstein's cell phone and explained the crisis. "Bernie, the girl needs help— right away!"

"Give me the address. I'll take care of it."

"CAN DO, BERNIE," Scarlotti responded on his cell. "Me and Mike are working tonight. We'll handle the wife-beater, and then we'll check out the pain doc. No sweat."

Joseph Battaglia parked the van. Leaning on his cane, he limped after his partner to the front entrance. Scarlotti rang the bell and pounded on the front door. They heard muted screams coming from inside. No one answered. Battaglia banged his solid oak cane hard against the door, yelling, "Police! Open up. Police!"

A yellow porch light flickered. Someone stared through the peephole. The chain was unlatched; a big guy loomed at the door.

He was thick all over and heavily muscled, with blond, crew cut hair. "Who the fuck are you guys?"

"Special police deputies. Does Joyce Gatlin live here?"

"None of your goddamn business. Get lost, you old farts."

Battaglia swung his cane fast and hard, connecting with the bridge of the man's nose. Blood splayed off. Gatlin's legs gave out from under him. Reaching down, Battaglia jerked him hard into the air with one hand, bringing Gatlin's face next to his. "Be nice to your lady, understand?" With his other hand, Battaglia sent his cane crashing into Gatlin's kneecap. The cane hit his leg with a sickening crunching sound. Gatlin grabbed at his broken kneecap, shrieking in pain.

Sal Scarlotti kicked Gatlin hard in the groin. "Sir, if we receive any further reports of bad behavior, or if you report this to anyone, we'll be back. Next time we won't be so polite. *Capiche?*"

"IT'S MY TURN. Let's visit the pain doctor." Scarlotti glanced at his watch: 2 A.M. "Go past Kmart; hang a right on Virginia; Ocala is on the left."

The pain management facility was a tidy, landscaped, one-story, brown clapboard building. "Park next door in that dental clinic parking lot," Scarlotti directed. "Wait and keep an eye out." He lifted a plastic bag and gas container from the vehicle, moved silently to the building's back entrance, pulled on latex gloves, and inserted a metal device. Easing open the door, Scarlotti disconnected the alarm. Using a pen flashlight, he studied the doctor's office. He pulled down patients' file folders from ceiling-high racks, pushing them into three-foot high piles in the center of the building. Crazy Sal Scarlotti carefully poured gasoline over the paper and cardboard folders. Reaching into the plastic bag, he withdrew three small explosive charges and a remote-controlled detonator. Then he returned to the van.

Joseph Battaglia pulled out of the dental clinic parking lot. They were half a block away when Scarlotti pressed a remote control button hidden in his windbreaker pocket. The blast roared like mortar rounds exploding, followed by the sound of glass shattering. They could see bright orange-red flames and smoke billowing skywards. Burning embers of paper and cardboard drifted down like snow.

The distant howls of sirens were heard heading towards the blaze—shrill, pulsating wails growing in intensity. "Let's get some coffee and donuts," Battaglia suggested. "There's an all night place out Virginia Avenue past I-95."

...15

Police Investigate Pain Clinic Fire

FORT PIERCE—Arson is suspected in the fire on Ocala Avenue that totally destroyed the pain management clinic of Dr. Elliot Summers. No arrests have as yet been made. Police are continuing to investigate the case that officers conclude might be gang-related. Patients interviewed reported that Summers was a wonderful doctor who gave out prescriptions for Oxycodone and Oxycontin whenever requested, with no questions asked. Efforts to contact Dr. Elliot Summers have been unsuccessful.

...16

THE APRIL MORNING dawned drab and sunless. There had been heavy showers in Washington during the night. Latisha entered Nurkiewicz' office carrying two coffees. Fernandez felt a slight bulge in his pants gazing at the girl's large dark eyes, full lips, curved hips and full breasts. As she put his cup down, her breast grazed against his shoulder with the flash of a knowing smile.

Nurkiewicz digested the Rothstein report he had received from the FBI office in Fort Pierce. The muscles of his jaw bulged as he finished the first folder. "I knew it. Bernie Rothstein is setting up an operation in Fort Pierce. Read this."

Joseph "Bats" Battaglia served as top enforcer for the Ozone Park Boys, a Gambino crime family based in Queens run by Leo Lasasso. The Ozone Park Boys ran a $30 million-a-year sports gambling enterprise. In 2000, Lasasso was arrested for failing to file New York tax returns and sent away. Bats Battaglia was never brought up on charges. They called Battaglia the "crippler." He killed with hammers, slappers and blackjacks, but Battaglia was a loyal Yankees fan, and baseball bats were his favorite.

Nurkiewicz sighed. After handing the Battaglia file to Fernandez, he opened the second folder, studying the head shot of a frail-looking man with neatly combed white hair, a thin mustache and thick glasses.

Salvadore "Crazy Sal" Scarlotti has expertise in guns, hand grenades and explosives. Reputed to be a dangerous, out-of-control, bona-fide psychopath without conscience or scruples.

41

Scarlotti worked for the Connecticut faction of the Sicilian mob.
He has no outstanding warrants.

"That's how Scarlotti's connected to Rothstein," Nurkiewicz muttered. "Who's next, Genghis Khan?" He picked up a colored photograph of Edward Rizzo, a short, bony man in his seventies with curly black hair and pale skin.

Edward "Fast Eddie" Rizzo: Started as small time pickpocket and petty thief. Joined the LoCascios' Bronx faction in 1995 and was convicted for plotting the robbery of an armored car at a bank in Marlboro, New York, and a break-in at the Long Island home of the late Outfit boss Rocky LaPietra. After serving five years in the super-max prison in Marion, Illinois, and not ratting anyone out, Edward Rizzo was paroled and is now residing in Florida.

Silence claimed the room. Fernandez's mind fogged as he reviewed the final folder Nurkiewicz handed him.

Michael De Luca: "Big Mike" De Luca worked for the Dasso Crew, headed by Capo Pauli Dasso and Soldier Roy DeMarco, the most ruthless of all the Gambino crew leaders. The FBI believes De Luca to be responsible for hundreds of executions. The real number will never be known, because there are no traces of the victims. Body parts were either sent to landfill sites or dumped at sea. De Luca was the principal suspect in the Hoffa murder, but there was never a body.
A Mafia underboss named Lefty Carnaggio talked to federal agents in 2007, attempting to cop a plea on an unrelated charge. Under oath, Carnaggio swore that De Luca hid Hoffa's body in a steel drum and buried it. Later,

when things quieted down, De Luca dug it up and placed it in the trunk of a car that was smashed down to a four-by-two cube of metal in a giant car compressor. The car with Hoffa's remains, along with hundreds of other com-pacted cars, was believed to have been shipped to Japan to be used in the making of new cars.

"Hoffa is part of a Toyota somewhere," Nurkiewicz shrugged. "That's yesterday's news. What we have here is proof that Rothstein has assembled a crew of stone-cold killers for his brother-in-law."

Fernandez read aloud, "These four Mafioso plus Rothstein took control of a security services business in Fort Pierce called the Orange Blossom Security Agency." He raised his eyebrows. "And their company has a contract with the city of Fort Pierce to assist in crime prevention."

"Orange Blossom Security Agency, my ass," Nurkiewicz muttered. "They should be called the Orange Blossom Mob."

Fernandez flipped through the final comments. "Wolffe has been photographed going into the St. Lucie County Library in down-town Fort Pierce. He goes there twice a week at the same time."

Nurkiewicz peered closely at photographs of men and women entering the library. "The whole thing is perfect cover for his mob's activities. What about Wolffe's wife?"

"You won't believe it."

"Try me."

"Rosalie Wolffe works in the state attorney's office."

Nurkiewicz made a fist. "I sniffed it from the start. The Mafia is taking over Fort Pierce." His eyes flashed. Controlling a grin, he added, "This is big. Really big!"

...17

FERNANDEZ TOOK OFF HIS JACKET with one hand, then peeled off the shoulder holster and slung it across the back of his chair. His 900-square-foot apartment on Connecticut Avenue looked disheveled: dirty dishes stacked in the sink, bed not made, white shirts to be taken to the dry cleaner in a pile near the entrance. A week's worth of dirty laundry lay on the floor in front of the washer-dryer.

He ignored the answering machine's flashing yellow light, turned on the television, kicked off his shoes, poured a drink and swirled his scotch while listening to the ice rattle. His cell phone jangled. He balanced his glass, dragged the phone from his pocket, opened it one-handed and listened.

"I found out something about Marcus Wolffe that will surprise you."

"Meet me at Chiang's Restaurant. Four-thousand block, Connecticut Avenue, one hour." Fernandez hung up smiling.

TO THE WAITRESS HE SAID, "The liquid of the gods—sake, please. Hot."

"I'll have the same," Latisha added.

"Tell me why you are were so excited on the phone."

She took a sheaf of laser-printed papers and spread them across the table. "Marcus Wolffe's computerized medical records."

"Okay."

"He was hospitalized in Kentucky in August 2004."

"The General Tso's chicken is excellent," he suggested. "Go on, I'm listening."

The sake arrived. Latisha lifted the tiny white porcelain cup and wrinkled her nose. "Smells like jet fuel."

44

"An acquired taste."

"I Googled Marcus Wolffe's name and got twenty hits. One reported a survivor of a plane crash in March 2006 during a major snowstorm at Bluegrass Airport, Lexington, Kentucky. A Canadair Jet flight from Chicago used the wrong runway for landing; pilot error. The aircraft overran the short runway and crashed, killing 45 passengers and three crew members. Two people survived. One died in the hospital. The other passenger was identified as Marcus Wolffe."

Fernandez downed another sake. "Lucky guy."

"I'm getting to the good part. I ran a software program comparing the data we have collected. Out popped a variance. The blood type on Marcus Wolffe's Army discharge papers was listed as Type O, and the blood type on his Kentucky hospital medical records is listed as A positive."

"Ah. So. Therefore, as a lawyer you contend that the man who boarded the flight in Chicago was not the same man who survived it. Correct?"

Latisha nodded sheepishly.

"Do you have any idea that statistically, over 100,000 people *die* each year from mistakes that occur in hospitals? Obviously, these errors are rarely publicized and often hidden from patients' family members to avoid lawsuits. And, remember, these 100,000 mistakes are fatalities. The frequency of clerical errors must be enormous. Sorry to burst your balloon."

She looked down at her plate, pushing the rice around absently with her fork. "Don't you think the blood variance thing is a little coincidental?"

Fernandez sensed her disappointment. "Latisha, I admire your initiative. I do. But please get coincidence out of your mind. It is a luxury term used by civilians to explain things away. In the FBI, we operate in a sometimes lawless and violent world where coincidence doesn't count."

She continued to stare at her plate.

"There really was once a General Tso," he explained, trying to lighten the mood. "A 19th century military leader from Hunan province named Tsung-t'tang Tso. After each military victory, his wife would make this dish for his officers—"

"I mentioned the blood thing to Daddy," she interrupted. "He thought that it merited looking into."

Fernandez' face reddened. "I know I didn't show appreciation for your initiative. I apologize for that. But I have to tell you straight out. If everything we discuss gets reported to your daddy, then you're not an FBI intern; you are nothing but a snitch. I already have more trouble in my life than I can handle—more I don't need. Go home, girl; let me enjoy my rice wine in peace."

Latisha didn't move. She had a stricken look on her face and reached over and took Fernandez' hands in hers. "You are right, Frank," she stammered. A tear crept into her eye. "I acted childishly in order to get my father's approval. Forgive me. It won't happen again."

He gazed at the achingly beautiful black lady holding his hands. "I have a suggestion. From now on, let's try and be more professional. What goes on in the FBI stays in the FBI. OK?"

"Yes. Saint Fernandez?"

He ignored the barb. "In return, I will try to get you transferred from being Nurkiewicz' secretary—"

"Administrative professional assistant."

"Whatever. Maybe I'm wrong and you're right. Let's turn this Wolffe blood variance into a positive learning experience for you. Contact the local papers that covered the crash. See if you can locate any reporters who were around at the time and are cooperative. Track down the passengers seated near Wolffe. With multiple broken bones, he wouldn't have had time to roam around the plane. Theoretically, if there *were* any switching of identities, it would have occurred immediately after the crash. That's your homework assignment."

Latisha stood up to leave. She smiled. "Friends?"

He watched her sashay around tables on the way out, garnering appreciative male gazes the whole way. Fernandez understood that he had allowed sexual feelings to intrude into his professional relationship with an intern. *Clinton got himself impeached for having sex with an intern.* He sighed regretfully, thinking of Latisha's lush body. He also realized that if he messed with Latisha Du Burns, her congressman father had enough juice to have him exiled to Gitmo, have him water boarded and probably castrated.

His cell phone jangled.

"Glenner approved my increased staffing request—on a temporary basis," Nurkiewicz told him. "I've transferred Charlie Manion to D.C. He's on the team."

Fernandez had a tight feeling in his chest. "Are you sure you want to do this, Dick?" he asked in an urgent whisper. "You know Manion and I don't—"

"Yes, it is exactly what I want to do," Nurkiewicz repeated, cutting him off. "Manion has an outstanding performance record. He will be a valuable addition to this investigation."

"What I'm saying is that Manion and I have a history. I don't think—"

"I don't care if you two don't like each other. Find a way to work together. My office, ten o'clock." Nurkiewicz hung up.

He signaled the waitress. "Another hot sake, please. No. Make it a double."

...18

"A WORD OF WARNING," Nurkiewicz pointed out. "Spilled blood and dead bodies increase newspaper and TV ratings. You people are not to talk to *anyone*. I'll handle all media communications. Understood?"

Fernandez nodded, steeling himself for a difficult meeting.

"Good. That means I will not have to worry about picking up the *Washington Post* or watching the *Morning Show* on Fox." He looked at his watch and cleared his throat for silence. "Latisha has requested assignment to the team. She signed a non-disclosure agreement, hardly necessary considering her father's prominence.

"Okay," Nurkiewicz continued. "I will turn the meeting over to Fernandez and leave you people to it. Investigate Wolffe and his Orange Blossom Mob. Let's try and prevent a Florida Mafia war, people." Looking directly to Fernandez: "You uncover anything that I should know about, you call me. Any time."

After he left, Fernandez looked at Manion. "You know what he's doing, don't you? He thinks we are so pissed at each other that we can't work together. Meantime, nothing gets accomplished, and if there is an outbreak of Mafia violence in Florida, then Nurkiewicz regains his power and staffing."

Manion smirked. Latisha looked confused.

"Well, it's not going to happen." Fernandez gave Manion a hard look. "If I offended you years ago by doing something stupid, let it go. This Mafia business could be serious, or it could be a Nurkiewicz wet dream. Either way, we are going to do our job. That's all I care about." He held Manion's eyes until he saw a slight nod of agreement.

"WHO IS MARCUS WOLFFE?" Fernandez wrote with a black marker pen on an easel flip chart. "What facts do we know? No guesswork. Latisha, you have his discharge papers? Fill us in. Age?" Fernandez asked.

She read, "Born seven April 1947, age 65, but when I saw him outside the restaurant—"

"Just facts, please."

"Place of birth reads Homestead, Florida."

"How about family information from his birth certificate?" Manion asked.

"Wolffe's birth records were destroyed in a hurricane."

"Sounds phony."

Fernandez said, "Do we have his civilian occupation?"

"A greeting card salesman. According to Marcus Wolffe's discharge papers, his last employer is listed as Norcross Greeting Card Company, West Chester, Pennsylvania."

Charlie Manion tapped on his iPad. "Norcross went out of business in the '80s."

"Physical data?"

Latisha smiled. "Army records list him as a blood type O, blue eyes, height 71 ½, weight 170, single."

"Date and entry into the service?"

"Sixteen March 1968. Philadelphia, Pennsylvania."

"Honorably discharged?" Manion asked.

"Yes, Wolffe served in the Vietnam War as a multimedia illustrator. He produced visual displays and documents."

"What about the difference in blood types?" Latisha said.

"Different blood types?" Manion raised his eyebrows.

Fernandez explained. "Latisha uncovered a blood variance that should be checked out. Marcus Wolffe survived an Air Canada plane crash about six years ago. His flight left Chicago bound for Dallas, ran into a major snowstorm and was diverted to Lexington, Kentucky. Unfortunately, the pilot tried to land the aircraft on a runway designated for small private planes. He didn't make it. Forty-nine people died in the crash. Wolffe received multiple fractures and facial nerve damage. Latisha did a computer program analysis and found that the man's Lexington hospital blood type and Army discharge blood types were not the same. The Army says he's type O, and the Kentucky hospital records list Wolffe as being blood type A positive."

"Hospitals are cutting staffs to save money," Manion remarked. "Probably a clerical error."

Latisha opened a folder and withdrew several papers. "Frank wanted me to locate reporters who covered the crash. In six years there have been staff reductions and job turnovers. I found someone who worked for the *Lexington Herald-Leader*. His name is Ross McCauley. McCauley was alerted by his editor and drove his four-wheel SUV through the snowstorm. He told me that when rescuers reached Canadair Flight 652, it was already an inferno. One fireman received third-degree burns on his arms dragging two survivors from the cracked cabin. Flames prevented rescuers from reaching anyone else on board. McCauley faxed me his article from the paper." She handed out copies.

Plane Crash Kills 49; One Survivor

LEXINGTON HERALD-LEADER, MARCH 15, 2006—
Air Canada's Flight 652 from Chicago destined for Dallas, Texas, was diverted because of severe weather conditions and advised to land at Lexington's Bluegrass Airport. In the heavy snowstorm and predawn darkness, the pilot unsuccessfully attempted to land the Canadair Regional Jet CRJ-900 on the shortest runway at the Lexington airport.

The 3,500-foot-strip was reported to have been unlit and barely half the length of the airport's main runway. The plane plowed through a perimeter fence, crashed in a field less than mile from the end of the runway, then burst into flames. Forty-nine people were killed. Two passengers were rescued and taken to University of Kentucky Hospital in critical condition.

The plane had undergone routine maintenance as recently as Saturday and had 14,500 flight hours, "consistent with aircraft of that age," a representative of Air Canada reported. Investigators from the FAA and NTSB were at the scene. The airline announced that they were attempting to contact relatives of the passengers.

"Not much there we didn't know," Fernandez said.

"The reporter told me that Air Canada worked around the clock trying to contact relatives of the passengers. Even though all the names received national media coverage, he thought it odd that no friends, family or business associates ever contacted the hospital regarding the victims."

Manion asked, "How extensive were the injuries?"

She referred to her papers. "Mr. Wolffe suffered serious facial nerve damage, in addition to multiple broken bones and amnesia. The doctors reported that the survivor evidenced no memory of the crash or the events leading up to it."

"And the other passenger?"

"The second survivor died. No explanation given."

Fernandez went to the easel and flipped over a new sheet. "Let's continue with the second key question we should be asking ourselves." He wrote "WHY?"

"Why was the guy in Chicago? Why was he leaving the country? Why did he steal Marcus Wolffe's identity? Why did he move to Baltimore?" He furrowed his brow. "And why suddenly emerge as a Mafioso?" Fernandez looked around the table. "Any other key questions that we should be asking ourselves?" No one responded.

"Manion, you know how to cut through red tape. Contact Air Canada and request an urgent response to the following questions: How was Wolffe's ticket paid for? Cash or charged? If charged, what credit card company? Did he leave a local contact number in Chicago? And what was his flight origination point and final flight destination?

"Latisha, I want you to check out Chicago area newspapers. Other than the big snowstorm, were there any unusual occurrences reported in the media a day or two before the Air Canada flight?"

Fernandez stood up and stretched to ease the sharp ache in his chest. He needed a caffeine fix, but couldn't stomach Latisha's coffee. "Let's take a break." He slipped out to the cafeteria.

THIRTY MINUTES LATER, after they had reassembled, Latisha reported. "Other than the big snowstorm, nothing much going on in Chicago during that period."

"Fine," Fernandez agreed. "Let's move on to—"

"I also checked newspapers in nearby cities," Latisha added, eyes focused on her laptop. "I don't know whether this is relevant: The *Milwaukee Journal Sentinel* ran a feature on March 12th about a crooked insurance executive gunned down in a local restaurant." She read, " 'Abe Dorfman, scheduled to be the principal witness to testify in a federal grand jury probe of organized crime and mob infiltration of Las Vegas.' "

Manion tinkered with his laptop. "Milwaukee is an hour and a half from Chicago, and they didn't get heavy snow until March 13th. What do we have here—a hitman?"

A look of tired amusement flickered across Fernandez' face, but he stifled it. "What we need is evidence, not wild suppositions. Evidence." He stood up and stretched. He rolled his head from side to side to stimulate circulation, then backwards until he felt his neck crack.

"Wolffe worked in Pennsylvania and got discharged from the Army in Pennsylvania. Why did he go to Baltimore?"

Manion shrugged. "Crab cakes? Ravens? Orioles?" He looked at Fernandez. "Maybe a woman?"

"I don't think that it was a financial move," Latisha said. "Wolffe opened an account in a BankAmerica branch in Pikesville, Maryland in 2007. No unusual or suspicious transfers, according to the branch manager. After he married, he made it a joint account."

Manion looked at his watch. "Nurkiewicz wants me located in Washington for a while. I have to check into my hotel. Besides, we're not getting anywhere. I don't even know what this character looks like."

Latisha turned to her laptop, to which she had attached a mouse. Fernandez realized this young woman was one of those young people born after his time who had been weaned on computers and found their inner workings understandable. She moved it with her hand, and Manion viewed photos of Marcus Wolffe taken in Baltimore and Fort Pierce. Fernandez stood over her shoulder as she clicked through the stream of pictures. Pointing to one taken outside the restaurant in Little Italy, Manion said, "I remember that shot of him coming out of the restaurant."

"He looks more than sixty-five," Latisha commented.

Fernandez watched idly as Latisha showed pictures of Wolffe in Fort Pierce entering and leaving the library. She clicked again. "He goes there on Tuesdays and Thursdays like clockwork."

"Who are all the old people?" Manion asked.

Fernandez said, "Stephen King wrote, 'Florida is for the newly wed and nearly dead.' All the young people are working."

"Here he is shopping at Publix with his wife," Latisha said. "And here he is walking on the beach." She flashed Wolffe talking to an old wrinkled-face fisherman wearing a battered Army cap.

His angular face resembled a bird on lookout. "On this next one he's going into the health club."

"Looks in good shape for an old guy," Manion quipped.

Fernandez stiffened. "Manion, go on, check in to your hotel. I have a doctor's appointment this afternoon."

"Something serious, I hope," Manion snickered as he left.

Latisha showed concern. "Health problem?"

"Long story." Fernandez massaged his aching chest.

"What's wrong?"

He ignored her question. "Run that picture of Wolffe on the beach again. That's it. Hold it there, where he's talking to the fisherman." The picture appeared gray and milky, and the detail definition was soft. The crook of the man's nose and the cut of his jaw reminded Fernandez of a hawk.

"Can you enlarge it? Good." He squinted at the screen for a long time, trying to work out who it could be. He had a vague feeling he recognized the man. Had he met him before, and if so, in what connection? He searched his memory, but in vain. Then it hit Fernandez like a punch in the chest. He heaved a weary sigh, put his head in his hands and breathed heavily.

"What in the world is the matter with you?"

"The photo of Marcus Wolffe with the man on the beach. I recognize that wrinkled, hawk face. I heard him lecture at Quantico. The man Wolffe's talking to is Alexander Lindsay. Lindsay is the head of the CIA's Black Ops, the codename for our government's covert, clandestine activities."

Latisha didn't answer, only stared at him.

The physical reality of the photograph made him queasy. "In the FBI, we call Lindsay's people the 'Good Assassins.' I need you to make me a copy and then delete the fisherman's picture from all files." He handed Latisha a flip phone, black, a little larger than the standard cell phone.

"What's this?"

"A cold phone, encrypted and routed through proxies. From now on, until I tell you otherwise, use only this phone. One more thing, Latisha. You do not discuss this man in the photo with your father. I'm serious. If you did, both of your lives could be in danger. Everything we do from here on out is under the radar. Understood?"

"You're scaring me."

He managed a sad smile. "I'm scaring myself."

FERNANDEZ SHOVED HIS GUN AND HOLSTER into his top desk drawer and left the J. Edgar Hoover Building, walking south on 9th Street two blocks to Pennsylvania Avenue and the headquarters of the U.S. Department of Justice. The photograph was stored in his briefcase. Flashing his badge, Fernandez passed through the electronic screening and took the elevator to the fifth floor, where the offices of USNCB were located. The National Central Bureau was the official U.S. representative to the International Crime Police organization, Interpol.

"*Buenos días*, handsome," whispered the attractive woman with glossy dark brown hair, caramel-brown eyes and a sharp nose. "Why did you stop calling me, big guy?" She gave him a wounded expression, pouting her lips.

"Darlene, I need a favor."

"Have I ever refused you anything, Frank honey?"

"I'm looking for a confirmed photo-match of this suspect, whether he's alive, dead or missing. Here's his photograph. Use your USNCB contacts and rush this through the Interpol database. I know these requests take time, but I need it as fast as possible, and completely off the record."

She stared straight back at him. "How about buying me a drink after work?"

"I'd love to," he lied, "but I have a doctor's appointment in Baltimore."

"If it's nothing communicable," she winked, "call me."

"STEP ON THE SCALE and have a seat, please," the nurse ordered, making an entry on his chart. She took Fernandez' blood pressure and raised her eyebrows. "One eighty over a hundred."

"Problem?" he asked.

"I'd work on it if I was you. Best talk to Dr. Fernandez. You two related?"

"We're twins, separated at birth. We haven't seen each other in over forty years."

'That's nice," she mumbled in a flat, disinterested voice, guiding him to a cul-de-sac of antiseptically white examining rooms on the fifth floor of Johns Hopkins Outpatient Center. "In here. Take off everything above your waist. Put on this gown. Doctor will see you soon."

MARTIN FERNANDEZ looked up from the chart and shook his head. Despite a broad stomach and thinning black hair, the doctor was a young-looking fifty-five. "Pressure's way up and you've gained too much weight." He flashed a small light into his brother's eyes. "Pupils dilated. Talk to me, Frank. Are you depressed? Sleeping okay?" When he didn't get a response, he continued, "Let me examine your chest. How is the wound healing? Is it tender when I press?"

Fernandez flinched, but remained silent.

His brother looked at his nose. "What happened?"

"I'm accident prone."

Martin Fernandez shook his head. "I want you to stop on the first floor before you leave and have a blood test and x-rays." He jotted a prescription. "Frank, I've done some research on retained bullet fragments. Tens of thousands of gunshot victims have lead levels high enough to pose serious threats. Even though we got most of the metal slivers out, I still want to keep a close eye on it. Despite the absence of symptoms, patients carrying lead bullet fragments in their bodies need to be aware of the signs of lead intoxication. Believe me, it could be serious."

He touched Frank's shoulder. "You paid your dues. You were shot twice and nearly died. You may even have lead poisoning. Don't you ever think about quitting?"

"Every day," Fernandez answered. "But what I would do?"

"With your skill set, you could work for any security company in the country."

"I don't know whether you can understand, Martin." He took a deep breath. "In many ways, this is still a closed society, an Anglo-Saxon country of pale, right-wing bigots fearful that Hispanics will have lots of babies and will take over their country. Sometimes I think the Bureau reflects the right wing's conservative views. We represent sixteen percent of the population, but only seven percent of FBI personnel are Hispanic."

"I fail to see the connection."

"I fucked up an important drug bust, Martin. Don't think that my being Hispanic went without notice or comment. I can't leave under that cloud."

The doctor tightened his lips, shrugged and didn't respond.

Fernandez' phone chirped. "I better get it, Martin. Sorry."

"Frank, it's Latisha. You wanted to know why Wolffe would choose to go to Baltimore after his plane crash. Johns Hopkins is rated the number one hospital in the country, according to *U.S. News and World Report*."

"Thanks. I'll call you back." Turning to his brother, he said, "I need a favor, bro. Check the hospital's patient data bank for me?"

Martin Fernandez looked at his watch. "I can't. I won't, and I'm running late for my appointments. Hasn't the FBI ever heard of the AMA's Code of Medical Ethics? Information disclosed during the course of the patient-physician relationship is confidential to the utmost degree."

"It's related to an investigation, Martin."

"Please don't pull that Patriot Act crap on me."

"It's important——to me. Please."

Dr. Fernandez sat at the computer. "Who and when?"

"Marcus Wolffe, between 2006 and 2007."

"I don't know if patients' records were computerized that far back." He fingered computer keys, rapidly scrolling down long lists. "Here we go. Wolffe, Marcus, age 59. Admitted following serious airplane accident. Dr. Elaine Miller-Green performed the operation. Miller-Green is double board certified. She's the best." He peered closer to the screen. "The otolaryngology surgery was successful. OK, Frank, satisfied?"

"What's otolaryngology surgery?"

"Your patient had a face change."

... 20

THE BALTIMORE-WASHINGTON TRAFFIC frustrated Fernandez, maddening congestion everywhere. Long lines of red brake lights streamed ahead of him; long lines of bright white headlights streamed toward him. He drove east on New York Avenue to Massachusetts, feeling a stiffness at the base of his neck and a slow, steady throb in his right chest. Fernandez parked, entered the lobby and nodded to the old man behind the desk—who never looked up. *Terrific security.*

From the elevator Fernandez trudged down the long hallway to his apartment, unlocked the door, dropped his gun and holster on a chair, and went into the bathroom. After peeing and flushing, he downed four Tylenol tablets for his chest pain. He splashed water on his face and ran wet fingers through his hair.

He suddenly paused and sniffed: something was not right. The hair on his neck bristled. He had an adrenaline rush: someone else was in the apartment. His gun lay on the chair across the room. Taking a slow step toward his weapon, he paused, spying the figure reclining on his sofa, smiling up at him. "Latisha, how did you get in here?"

She held up a credit card. "I was a Girl Scout." She patted the cushion beside her and crooked a finger for him to come closer. "You frightened me today with that spooky Black Ops business. Daddy is in South Korea on a fact-finding mission. I am afraid to sleep alone in our house. I thought maybe—"

He gave a short laugh. "Stop right there. You're an intern. I am an over-the-hill FBI agent twenty years your senior."

Unruffled, she answered, "I heard that once you're over the hill, you begin to pick up speed."

"I'm happy to hear that. Out, young lady. Now!"

"No need to snap at me. I brought a bottle of sake."

60

Fernandez hesitated. He'd felt an erection just talking to her, listening to the sound of her voice. She drove him crazy: her eyes, her hair, imagining those dark nipples. He twisted open the sake lid and poured two small drinks.

"Latisha. Please listen to me. My record with the Bureau is shaky—at best. My last mission failed. Nurkiewicz keeps me for one reason: the FBI director and I served in the Marines together. I'm only human; you're a beautiful, desirable woman. If word ever got out that you spent the night here, I'm toast. Can you understand?"

At this, Latisha began to laugh. "Did Goodwill do your decorating?" She glanced around the apartment: wood floors, a frayed oriental carpet, used furniture. A small television set with a big cable box wired to it. Some books on a shelf; a small music system with a pile of CDs propped against it. She studied the silver-framed photograph of a woman.

Fernandez spoke in a tight voice. "Being married to an FBI agent is not easy on a marriage. The pretty blond in the picture is my ex-wife, Ashley. After 9-11, all Bureau personnel were on duty or on call 24/7. I couldn't handle the late hours and travel without feeling guilty or constantly having to apologize; definitely not the kind of relationship Ashley had expected." He sipped the sake again.

"I don't see a photograph of Mrs. Manion."

Fernandez shifted in his chair, looking down at the floor. "Inexcusable behavior. Clara was my wife's best friend; Charlie, a colleague. I became depressed after my divorce—drinking too much, not eating. Clara invited me to their house for dinner. Manion was on the West Coast on a special assignment. Clara and I were both lonesome. One thing led to another. It didn't last long—lust, not love. The Manions patched things up, the way people do. They have three kids and live in Annapolis."

Fernandez shrugged, downed the last of the sake and wondered if Manion would ever get the bitterness out of his system. If not, he couldn't blame him. He felt exhausted from the tedious drive and light-headed from mixing pills and alcohol. "I need black coffee," he mumbled as the phone rang.

"I'll get it," Latisha volunteered.

"Noooo," Fernandez slurred.

She had already picked up the receiver. "Hello."

"Latisha Du Burns, is that you? What in the hell are you doing in Fernandez' apartment? Put him on," Nurkiewicz barked.

She slapped her forehead, silently mouthing, "*Sorry!*"

"Look, Richard," Frank muttered. "Nothing is—"

"Don't 'Richard' me, Fernandez. You sound drunk. Are you out of your fucking mind? Her old man controls our appropriations." Nurkiewicz paused, breathing heavily. "Get that girl out of your apartment ASAP! That's an order. Do you understand what I'm telling you?"

"I think so." Fernandez blinked, his vision fading fast, his tongue heavy. The phone dropped to the floor as he lost consciousness, dreaming of unfastening Latisha's black brassiere.

FERNANDEZ AWOKE WITHOUT REMEMBERING that he'd passed out. Strong sunlight streamed through the leaded glass windows. His telephone buzzed incessantly. Fernandez dragged it to his ear. "Yeah?"

"How you feelin' this morning?" Latisha chirped.

Frank squinted at his watch: 7 A.M. He couldn't focus.

"Mr. N. is asking for you; best get your sorry ass moving."

Through a twinge of pain, he saw that he was naked and in a mussed-up bed. Who had moved him to the bedroom and undressed him? He groaned, his voice still thick with sleep. "Did we—"

"Did we make like bunny rabbits and do the dirty deed? No, honey. If we had, I guarantee you would remember." She paused. "I never saw a man with four nipples before."

Fernandez gave a bleary smile. "I may be hung over," he growled. "But two of those nipples are bullet holes."

…21

"AIR CANADA REPORTED THAT Wolffe paid for his ticket with a Visa card," Charlie Manion informed Fernandez. "Starting point: Chicago; final destination: Dallas. I called Visa requesting an immediate update of his current statement. Visa charges are recorded instantly, so we know Wolffe stayed at the Chicago Hilton on March 13th and 14th. According to the hotel, he was attending the Housewares Show." Manion flipped another page. "He registered under his company name, MW & Associates. Specialty gift wrapping."

"Home address?"

"Hangzhou, China," Manion answered flatly.

Fernandez pondered the information. "Our man lives in China; he's a middleman for gift wrapping or whatever; travels to Chicago to work the Housewares Show." He idly reflected that international travel required a passport.

"Call the U.S. Passport Office. Have them fax a copy of Wolffe's passport and photo. I think they have a toll free number."

Latisha hunched over her laptop keys, fingers flying. "Try 877-910-7277."

Manion punched in the number. "This is a priority call from the FBI. Let me speak to your supervisor."

He held for a minute and winked at Latisha. "Hello. What's your name? Ned. Here's the scoop, Ned. I am Special Agent Charles Manion with the FBI in Washington. We are working an important case. Here are my shield and fax numbers. Jot them down. I need you to immediately fax a copy of the passport of a man named Marcus Wolffe. I believe that he is an American citizen living in Hangzhou, China—so it shouldn't be hard. And, Ned, I need it like yesterday. Got that, pal?"

Nurkiewicz entered without knocking. Jaw clenched, he glared angrily at Fernandez, who met his gaze and shrugged, deciding not to try and explain the previous night, not to make matters possibly worse.

"Latisha," Fernandez said. "Please see if the passport fax came in." Then he turned to Nurkiewicz. "Let me update you, Dick. Charlie's narrowed things down."

"We're getting a little closer," Manion explained. "Hard evidence of Wolffe being in Chicago in March. He stayed at the Hilton for two days and had airline tickets to Dallas before the crash. And then, I guess back home—to China."

"China? What the fuck does a Mafia character have to do with China? Is he connected to the Triads?"

Manion and Fernandez exchanged looks.

Latisha came in chuckling. She placed the faxed passport photo on the table. Manion picked it up. He gazed in open surprise. "This guy's bald as a turtle."

Fernandez laughed mirthlessly. "Well, we now know who Marcus Wolffe isn't."

"What the hell is going on?" Nurkiewicz demanded

Fernandez inhaled deeply, steadying his voice. "If I hadn't heard that Baltimore restaurant tape, I would never have believed Wolffe to be a syndicate godfather. It didn't compute: a Mafia mole working undercover for ten years, then suddenly surfacing to take over a crime syndicate—"

Nurkiewicz interrupted, his face beet red. "You don't know shit about the Mafia, Fernandez. Every operation you're involved in gets fucked up." He stared in open dislike. "You were accepted back from sick leave as a favor to your *Semper Fi* buddy, Glenner. But I can have you transferred to Alaska if you give me a reason to. So don't give me any more reasons. *Comprendes?*"

Fernandez blanched visibly. Embarrassed to be dressed down in front of Latisha, he clenched his teeth, cautioning himself not to respond while angry. He noticed the faint smile on Charlie Manion's face.

Nurkiewicz stormed out, slamming the door.

"What did he mean by Miami?" Latisha asked.

"I headed a failed drug bust a few years ago." His voice trailed off as he remembered the doctor saying, *"You may suffer pain from time to time, son. When the pains come, just thank God you can feel anything. You're lucky to be alive."*

"What exactly do we do now?" Manion grumbled.

Fernandez folded his arms. "Start over."

...22

"I CAN'T SEE FOR SHIT AT NIGHT," Eddie Rizzo groused. "The bright lights make it hard to make out street signs."

"Get the fuckin' cataract surgery," De Luca retorted. "In and out the same day, *bada bing bada boom*."

By 3 A.M. the street had quieted down. Integras and Accords, tricked out with aftermarket spoiler fins and alloy wheels, parked along the city's highest drug-trafficking area. A group of boys, school age, were sitting on the curb looking hard at the van.

"Hey, you kids," Rizzo shouted. "Get off the street. Stop pushing that shit." He pointed his finger like a gun. In return, one of the kids showed Eddie his closed fist with the middle finger extended upwards.

Three large, feral-looking black men approached the van. The leader wore a purple pinstriped suit jacket with black pants and a yellow, open-collar shirt. "You lookin' for some snatch, you ol' dawgs?"

"We are police deputies," Rizzo said. "From now on, no pushin' drugs on this street. Move your asses while you can."

"Hey now, you old mudderfuckers!" yelled the leader. His pupils were dilated, his movements awkward and slow. "Almost sounds like a threat, you understand what I'm talkin' about?"

Shaking his head, Eddie Rizzo got out of the van. De Luca followed. "Don't say you weren't warned."

"Fuck you, old man."

"Fuck me? No, fuck you, kid." Rizzo grinned at De Luca. "Like old times." Under the seat of the car, he had a snub-nosed 38. Eddie Rizzo grabbed it and shot the one in the purple pinstripe jacket squarely in the heart. The drug dealer went down, a finger of blood gushing in squirts from the dime-sized hole in his chest. Rizzo proceeded to shoot the other two dead, the report of each gunshot

67

muffled by the silencer. They stuffed the three bodies in the back of the van and drove slowly away.

"DOMESTIC VIOLENCE HOTLINE. Go ahead."

CALLER: "Are you the lady who helped Joyce?"

ROSALIE: "I believe so."

CALLER: "My name is Krystal."

ROSALIE: "OK, Krystal. What's the problem?"

CALLER: (Silence)

ROSALIE: "Are you still there, Krystal?"

CALLER: "My husband has been forcing himself on my daughter."

ROSALIE: "Do you mean sexually abusing her?"

CALLER: "He told me he would kill me if I called. He's done jail time."

ROSALIE: "Are you certain that he touched your daughter?"

CALLER: "*Touched* ain't the right word."

ROSALIE: "Give me your address, please."

CALLER: "He's got a swastika tattooed on his forehead."

ROSALIE: "That's nice."

DE LUCA'S CELL PHONE CHIMED. "OK. No problem, Bernie. Gimme the address. We still got room in the van."

Moonlight reflected off of the murky water running along the 10th fairway of the Gator Trace Golf Course. De Luca and Rizzo stepped out of their van and listened; all was quiet and still. No sound but the gentle stirrings of creatures in the water.

Big Mike De Luca played his flashlight over the water from side to side. Telltale spots of amber glowed where alligator eyes breached the surface. "There's one." Eddie pointed to a twelve-foot-long alligator nosing curiously out of the reeds and vines that trailed down from the 10th tee box. Rizzo got a glimpse of its wide, U-shaped, scaly snout and shivered.

"I always hit a slice on this hole," De Luca complained. "Because of the gators, I never go after the goddamn balls. Plus it costs me strokes."

The Orange Blossom men pulled the four bodies from the van, dragged them to the water's edge and dumped them in. Within seconds, convulsive slapping sounds came from the roiling water.

The swastika-tattooed child-molester was struggling in a frenzied state. His arms were securely bound with blue nylon rope. Two layers of duct tape across his mouth deadened his screaming.

Rizzo opened a switchblade and sliced the front of the man's jeans, exposing his genitals. "Now try molestin' the gators," Rizzo said as De Luca gently slid the big man into the dark water.

Never speeding, always carefully abiding by the traffic signs and lights on US-1, De Luca and Rizzo headed home.

Obesity Blamed in Death of Alligators

PORT ST. LUCIE—Dr. Mildred Matthews of the Fort Pierce Wild Animal Clinic reports that in her twenty-five years of practice on the Treasure Coast, she has never encountered this condition before in the genus of *Alligatoridae.* Dr. Matthews explained that alligators have strong immune systems and hardly ever get sick because their blood has proteins that produce antibiotics.

"The alligators that I examined at the Gator Trace Golf Course," Dr. Matthews adds, "were seriously overweight for their size and age. While most reptiles have three-chambered hearts, alligators and all crocodilians have four chambers. However, alligators were never intended to carry superfluous extra weight, which eventually leads to obesity, heart disease and death." Gator Trace golf officials have erected "No Feeding Alligators" signs at all water holes.

"I NEED COFFEE TO KEEP AWAKE," Bats Battaglia confessed. "Tell you the God's honest truth, Sal, I can't stay up late like I used to." A shiny black Lexus pulled into the all night Sunoco gas station. Music boomed from the car windows. One man crawled out of the car and stood by the air pump. He was tall, dark and lean, with an athlete's build. His flat-billed baseball cap was worn backwards; his pants were the hip-hop style that Vesta Jones had described. Behind the wheel, another man sat holding a lidded cup of Starbucks in one hand, and with his other he tapped out a beat on the steering wheel.

"That car has the drive-by shooter look," Scarlotti said. "A black Lexus with spinner wheels and blasting music."

Battaglia pulled up alongside. Sal lowered the window. "Turn down the music, pal. You're givin' me a headache."

The driver grinned arrogantly and laughed. "You got the Alzheimer's or some shit like that? How they let you out of the old age home? Fuck off!"

Scarlotti sighed. He lifted his snub-nosed .38 from beneath the seat and pointed it at their heads. "Pull over and park in front of Dunkin Donuts. Hands where I can see them. No sudden moves."

The two shocked young men kept their hands raised. Sal's eyes never left the driver, a slouchy black man wearing a visored cap pulled down over a bandana, a diamond stud in one ear and a patch of beard below his lip.

Crazy Sal reached into his van, removed a can of gasoline and ambled over to the Lexus. Methodically, he doused the hood and then emptied the gas can on the driver's front seat. He walked to the passenger window, reached into his pants pocket and pulled out a box of matches. He lit one and held it up.

"It's career-changing time, boys," he whispered, his thin lips hardly moving. And with that, Crazy Sal Scarlotti tossed the match into the Lexus window; flames burst up with a sudden rushing hiss. Thick black clouds of smoke poured from the windows as the drive-by shooting suspects ran off screeching. When the gas can exploded in a roar of metal and shrapnel, Scarlotti and Battaglia didn't flinch or look back; they continued on their appointed rounds as Partners on Patrol.

25

Hospital Issues Accident Advisory

FORT PIERCE—Officials at Lawnwood Regional Medical Center and Heart Institute report an alarming increase in adult men being admitted to the emergency room with broken or fractured kneecaps. Doctors say that this condition occurs when the triangle-shaped bone covering the knee (patella) is smashed, cracked or forced out of place.

According to the hospital's admission records, the primary cause of the recent rash of injuries reported was "Falling off of stepladders." Hospital officials are advising the public that because Fort Pierce has experienced an unusually high rainfall this summer, people should be cautioned against using metal ladders during lightning storms and not climbing wet and slippery ladders that may have been left out-of-doors in the rain.

...26

"GOOD NEWS AND BAD NEWS," Sergeant Vesta Jones announced from the podium. All five members of Orange Blossom Security Services perked up with interest. "You gentlemen may recall my mentioning Richie Sanford. We picked up the guy last night in an area where there were twenty robberies late at night. Richie's wearing dark clothes and he's carrying a screwdriver and flashlight. He lives ten miles away. We can't prove anything, and yet Richie just got out of jail for the same offense."

"Can we get one of them police radios?" Rizzo asked.

"In your dreams. We don't want you guys getting out of your vehicle, breaking a hip and suing the city. Remember what I told you. Your mission is to be a presence on the street, a crime deterrent. Understand?"

Fighting back a grin, Jones continued, "After an as-yet-unsolved explosion that totally destroyed a pain clinic that was on our watch list, it seems the prescription doctor involved is no longer residing in the area. At least, we can't locate him. This month's crime numbers are not out yet, but we believe that domestic violence, while on the rise nationally, is tailing down in Fort Pierce. Drive-by shootings are also down by a half, and drug activity on 23rd Avenue seems to be slowing down."

"Our compliments to you and your department, Sergeant," said Rothstein, the eighty-year-old disbarred lawyer.

"Our mayor is reporting these statistics to the media to prove that his strategy is working: utilizing volunteers to reduce the police force and costs. There's talk he intends to cut the force further." Jones shook her head in frustration. "The Lincoln Park gangs are our major cause of homicides in Fort Pierce. We would love to be able to identify budding gang members and encourage them to get out of the gangs, join the 5th Avenue Boys Choir, Police Athletic league, or get help learning to read—anything to try to lead a normal life."

"Tell us about these gangs," Rothstein persisted.

"Like most cities, we've got the Bloods and the Crips. We estimate the Bloods to have about one hundred members. They wear red shirts, caps and bandanas. The Crips wear blue. One gang gets angry with another gang, so they go into the other's neighborhood and kill somebody. People know RayRay or Pucci, or whoever did the killing, but because of community fear or apathy—nobody talks. People have friends or family and are afraid to testify. We might have suspects, but we can't prove a case with no physical evidence and no witnesses—just a dead guy and shell casings on the ground."

"How old are these punks?" Rizzo asked.

Jones shrugged. "The kids start at 12 years old, the enforcers 15-20, the OG's—"

Rothstein interrupted. "Who are OG's?"

"Original gangsters. They are retired from the everyday business, but like to drive around the hood in their Lincoln Navigators. These bozos carry Choppers and Gats, meaning assault rifles, handguns and shotguns."

"Still off-the-record," Rothstein said, "any suggestions?"

Vesta Jones gave the Orange Blossom men a hard stare. "You guys did good. Real good." She spoke firmly and seriously. "But you don't want to be messin' with these gangs, hear?"

...27

"WE ARE PROUD OF YOUR EFFORTS, Rosalie," said Jessica Towers, the state attorney serving the 19th Judicial Circuit of Florida. Jessica Towers had requested Rosalie's presence in her spacious office two floors below.

"I admire what you are doing to ease the pain of these poor abused women," Towers added, producing her automatic smile. "In recent weeks our Fort Pierce office has received a flood of favorable calls complimenting our Domestic Violence Hotline and singling your efforts, Rosalie, for special praise."

"My pleasure."

"People like you, Rosalie, have the God-given gift of empathy, of being a good listener, of being able to say the right things to help women over their difficulties. The work you are doing is important. *You* are making a difference."

"Thank you."

"I know that you will agree," Jessica Towers continued, "that there is no exercise better for the heart than reaching down and lifting people up."

"I suppose so."

"Rosalie, my dear, do you think that it would be possible to help us out one or two additional nights a week?"

"Could I get paid a little something for gas, or coffee and doughnuts?"

Abruptly, the state attorney rose from her chair and kissed Rosalie on her cheek. "I'm afraid not," she replied coolly. "Budget cuts and all that. Keep up the good work. Thanks for stopping by."

...28

THE COLOMBIAN DRUG LORD, Cezar Zúñiga, arrived promptly at one o'clock for his meeting with the Tampa mob boss, Peppe Palmisano. The Mafioso chief's manor house was situated on a rise in the center of a vast lawn. No shrubs had been allowed to grow in the front to prevent unwelcome visitors approaching from within three hundred yards of the house without being seen. Palmisano's residence resembled a fortress, with a high, electrified gate clotted with video cameras and a squawk box.

Zúñiga's driver and bodyguard sat stiffly in the front seat of the black Mercedes. The Colombian lowered the smoked-glass window and pressed the speaker button. He had bright blue eyes, a little hooded. "Please tell Don Peppe his guest has arrived."

After a few minutes, a black Cadillac appeared on the other side of the gate. Two burly men in dark suits, wearing shoulder holsters, approached the car. Zúñiga's gaze was direct and unflinching. He allowed himself to be frisked by the Italians and then bundled into the rear seat. The Cadillac reversed back up the long driveway, stopping beside the front entrance.

Palmisano's bodyguards guided Zúñiga along a stone walkway to a terrace surrounded by fruit trees. Out-of-season orange trees sprouted waxy, pointy, emerald-green leaves; peach trees drooped over with heavy, ripening fruit.

Peppe Palmisano had deep-set, heavy eyes and wore large black glasses. The tanned, wrinkled old Mafioso greeted his guest. The two men shook hands and kissed. "Come. Have a seat. A little Grappa, maybe?"

Zúñiga nodded.

"*Salute*," proposed Peppe, filling two small glasses. He opened his arms wide to encompass the fruit trees surrounding the terrace. "Every day fresh: grapefruit, November to March; oranges till May, and now," he squeezed three fingers to his lips and smacked, "and now, my peaches are in season."

The Colombian ignored Peppe's forced sociability. The Palmisano family ran the Tampa crimes syndicate, including extortion, shylocking, girls, drugs, and restaurant and bar supplies. Peppe Palmisano survived through predatory cunning, street acumen, guile and brutality. Whoever challenged his rule quickly disappeared.

Palmisano pushed his glass away and waved for coffee. "So, my friend, why you fly all the way from Colombia?"

Zúñiga proceeded cautiously. "Thank you for the Grappa. I believe that you will agree, Don Peppe, that my product is better and cheaper than the Mexicans'; it comes direct from the source, packed in hard bricks, never cut, 98 percent pure."

The Tampa boss nodded, waiting for Zúñiga to continue.

"My organization supplies one third of the cocaine on American streets, close to sixteen billion dollars a year. I have expensive overhead: a large payroll, drug labs in the jungle, and a submarine to transport drugs around the world." Zúñiga paused to let that information sink in. "As a businessman, Don Peppe, you can appreciate that I must protect my investment."

Palmisano answered with a hard silence. The Colombians were the go-to-guys for cocaine, brown heroin and prescription drugs, and they were not crazy, out-of-control cowboys like the Dominicans and Mexicans.

"Like any major consumer products organization," Zúñiga continued, "we wish to avoid media attention or government intervention. Am I perfectly clear on that point?"

Palmisano glanced at him sharply.

The Colombian held up both hands in a peaceful gesture. "I come as a friend, Don Peppe. We both have a problem that requires immediate resolution."

Palmisano knitted his brows, looking confused.

"I invest in information that could affect my business. And I've learned of a murder of a Casa Nostra boss up north—"

"Yeah, Fat Vinnie Gesumaria. So?"

"No disrespect, but you're not getting any younger, Peppe. According to my sources, a new *capo di tutti capi* is expanding his operation into Florida. A Mafia war would cause bloodshed and focus unacceptable attention on our operation." Zúñiga did not raise his voice or show any sign of emotion. "The new guy has to go. You do it, or we do."

Palmisano's eyes were hard to read behind the dark glasses. He could not permit the pockmarked Colombian with the big head to talk down to him, to disrespect him. Peppe shook his head with suppressed anger. "That's Mafia business—not yours. Someone tries to cut me out, I arrange to put a bullet in the fucker's head. And I got just the guy. "

TWO HOURS LATER, Peppe Palmisano picked up the phone and punched in a number. "Muscles, I got a job for you on the East Coast. This is an important piece of work. Here's all the information. Don't fuck up."

29

SIX FOOT FOUR, MICHAEL "MUSCLES" MARINARA drove east on Florida Route 70 in his bright red 1970 Chevrolet Chevelle convertible. The two hundred and fifty pound giant slapped his meaty palm against the side of his car, keeping time to Johnny Cash singing his favorite song.

When I was just a baby my mama told me. Son,
Always be a good boy, don't ever play with guns.
But I shot a man in Reno just to watch him die,
When I hear that whistle blowing, I hang my head and cry.

Muscles Marinara reached Federal Highway, then crossed the bridge spanning the Indian River. He didn't know what the mark had done. He didn't care. None of that was his business. The less he knew, the better. Marinara pulled over, rechecked the instructions that Peppe Palmisano had given him, then drove up to the guard-house.

"Yes sir?" the guard asked, holding a clipboard in his hand. The small guard had alert eyes, gray hair and a shiny forehead. "Who are you here to visit?"

Muscles forgot. He referred to his paper. "I'm eatin' lunch at the clubhouse."

"Sorry, sir, the Inn at Ocean Village is closed until the fall."

Irritated, Marinara squinted again at Peppe's information. "Well then, I'll just go to the Tiki Bar at the pool for a sandwich."

"Do you have your pink and white wrist band? Otherwise, it is beyond my authority to admit you."

Marinara's jaw muscles clenched into a knot. He reached under the driver's seat. He had in his hand a .357 Magnum.

"Listen to me, dickhead," Muscles muttered. "Open your fucking gate or I'll come to your house. I'll harm your wife and family. Understand? Even your pets."

The little guard blanched. He stumbled back, raising his hands. "They don't pay me enough to get involved in shit like this." He hesitated, then pushed the button to raise the gate.

Muscles Marinara lowered his weapon, gave the man a hard look, and shifted into drive. As his shiny red convertible started forward, the little guard suddenly depressed the gate button. Two hundred pounds of solid wood slammed down, penetrating Muscle Marinara's skull. His foot involuntarily hit the gas, and the Chevelle plunged ahead full speed into a drainage canal.

The guard punched in a number. "911? I want to report a vehicular driving fatality... and I need a tow truck."

...30

AT A LITTLE PAST SEVEN-THIRTY in the evening, Peppe Palmisano received news of the death of his hitman. Palmisano assumed Wolffe's Fort Pierce crew to be responsible for the whacking of Muscles Marinara. His heavy brow furrowed in thought; then bracing himself, he telephoned Carmine DeMimo, the New Jersey Mafia don and de facto head of the Commission of all northern crime families.

"Carmine," Peppe confided with a slight resignation in his voice, "I can't be letting this asshole think he can waltz into Florida and play us for fools. Word gets around on the street, we're out of business. I need your top gun. *Subito!*"

"*Col tempo la fogia di geiso diventa seta,*" DeMimo replied softly. "Time and patience change the mulberry leaf to satin." The New Jersey Mafia don added, "You only get what you pay for."

"Money is no object, Carmine." Peppe's voice sounded reedy; he paused for breath. "I also got the goddamn Colombians angling to take over my distribution. I don't need more problems."

"If you're good for fifty G's, I got your guy: George Fangman. The man's a predator, an efficient, cold-blooded killer."

"Is he Family?"

"No, but Fangman handled the heavy-duty contracts for New York and Jersey families. Grapevine gossip has it Fangman's killed over a hundred people."

"Have him contact me right away, Carmine."

"I'll try, but the guy may have retired. He's no kid; got a family and hates to travel. But with the economy, who knows? Be prepared, Peppe—the guy is scary-looking; a big motherfucker, goes over six-three. And he don't like meeting in daylight."

TWO NIGHTS LATER, in the dark parking lot outside a small Italian restaurant in Ybor City, Peppe Palmisano waited nervously, his hands jammed in his pockets. A large figure dressed entirely in black slowly emerged from the shadows, walking with a quiet, catlike gait, like a heavyweight prizefighter in his prime. In the yellow streetlight, Palmisano saw that the man had hooded, cold, flat, ice-colored eyes, like an animal that would readily tear open your throat.

"I don't talk in a car, on a cell phone or in a hotel room," Fangman told him. "Only walk-talks and at night. Nobody ever got locked up for a walk-talk. Let's go."

As the two men started down 7th Avenue, the Tampa Mafia boss wasted no time. "It's an honor to meet you," Peppe said nervously. "Your services to the New York families over the years are the stuff of legend."

Fangman's dead eyes showed nothing.

"The special piece of work involves hittin' a boss. You okay with that?"

"For the right price, I'll go see anyone."

Beneath his words, Peppe sensed a warning. "I need the job done quickly and untraceably," Peppe said. "The mark just moved into Fort Pierce. The guy's no pushover. There's fifty G's in it for you." Reaching into his inside pocket, Palmisano withdrew an envelope. "Here's the address, car make and license number. You sure you can handle it?"

With the barest glint of menace in his smile, Fangman replied, "Don't ask foolish questions." He handed Palmisano a slip of paper. "When you read about it in the newspapers, transfer the money to this bank account number. Are we done here?"

30

AFTER RICHARD "THE ICEMAN" Kuklinski's capture and sentencing to nineteen years in the New Jersey State Prison, George Fangman became the mob's number one assassin. When he entered a room, people looked away and spoke in respectful, hushed whispers. Fangman made people disappear with incredible cruelty, precision and expertise.

Before he made any kind of move, the master killer would survey an area for three or four days to determine his mark's daily routine. Fangman had a tried and proven method that he had used many times over. Once he learned when and where his target had gone, the killer would park his car as close to the mark's car as possible, get out, gave it a flat, then return to his van. He would sit and calmly wait for his victim to return. Fangman had unusual patience in these situations. Like a predator, he could sit still for hours on end.

The mark would come out, spot the flat, grumble, and open his trunk. As he bent over to pull out the spare tire, Fangman would steal up behind him and put a .38 in his lower back. "My friend, I need you to come with me," he would say, his voice faraway and detached. Fangman made the mark get in the trunk of his car on his stomach, after which he would handcuff him, tape his mouth shut and warn him to be quiet. Fangman then would close the car door, put the pistol under his seat, and drive off to a predetermined location to shoot the mark in the back of the head twice, then dispose of the body. If a cop pulled him over, he'd kill him. That simple.

"GOOD EVENING," George Fangman spoke pleasantly on the phone, "is Mr. Wolffe at home? This is the St. Lucie County tax appraiser's office calling."

"He's not here," Rosalie replied. "Can I help you?"

"Yes, ma'am. I'm calling to see if you have filed for your homestead real estate tax exemption. Many new Florida residents are unaware of the money you can save on your real estate tax bill by filing for the homestead exemption. We have representatives in Fort Pierce today and would be happy to meet with you and your husband to help you fill out the application."

"How considerate. My husband isn't at home, Marcus is at the library, but maybe I could—"

The line went dead.

AT 6 P.M. FANGMAN PARKED HIS STOLEN VAN next to the white Toyota Avalon. Ignoring the drenching rain, Fangman got out, rechecking Wolffe's tag number. He gave the car a flat, then walked calmly back to his van, switched off the engine and sat back to wait. When the target emerged from the library, he would get out of the car and come close to him. He did not plan to miss.

George Fangman checked his watch: 7:30. With the poor visibility, Fangman was prepared to call it a day, when squinting through the windshield, he observed a short man with a black umbrella walking slowly in his direction, avoiding puddle water. The umbrella obscured part of Marcus Wolffe's face.

Crossing the street to his car, Wolffe noticed the flat tire. Fangman moved quickly. He reached under the seat, withdrew his .38 Smith and Wesson revolver, and then slid silently out of the car. "Got a flat?" he asked, looking as if he cared, as if he were a Good Samaritan. "If you have a spare in the trunk, I can change it for you in no time."

Wolffe paused as if in deep thought, then looked up at his large benefactor. "Thank you. You are very kind." Marcus Wolffe shifted the umbrella to his left hand, fished for his keys, punched the trunk lid open, and reached inside for the tire iron. The van screened the two of them from view.

Fangman withdrew his .38 with a two-inch barrel, placing it in Wolffe's lower back. "My friend, I need you to come with me."

"You need to freshen your act, George."

"Huh?"

Wolffe slammed his tire iron into the killer's solar plexus. As Fangman gasped for air and bent forward, Wolffe cracked him hard with the edge of his hand at the juncture of neck and shoulder. The big man's knees buckled. In a split-second, Wolffe removed a jumper cable wire from the open trunk and tightened it around Fangman's neck until the killer dropped his gun and fell to his knees.

Shrouded in the rain and darkness, Wolffe grabbed him by the collar and dragged him to the van. "Who sent you, George?"

"Is that you, Uri?" Fangman mumbled, his blood-veined eyes wide in shock.

Wolffe tightened the cable wire. "Who sent you, George?"

Fangman understood the unspoken rules: no pleading, no repentance, no recourse. "Palmisano—Tampa," he whispered.

"Thank you, George," Wolffe answered, tightening the wire. Then he knelt next to the unconscious Mafia hitman, broke his neck, and hauled the dead body into the van.

...32

THE MORNING DAWNED a balmy, misty eighty degrees, about average for early summer in Tampa. Peppe Palmisano awoke in a testy mood; two days had elapsed and nothing had appeared in the newspapers. He barked breakfast orders to his Hispanic maid, Lupe, and strolled out onto his terrace for breakfast.

Palmisano's two sullen bodyguards looked like half-awake professional wrestlers stuffed into black business suits. As was his custom each morning, Peppe walked over to pick a ripe peach for his breakfast. Through the mysterious veil-like mist, he noticed a form free-floating on the peach tree. Still groggy from lack of sleep, Peppe moved closer for a clearer look. The form had the color and shape of an over-sized peach, but when he got close, he cringed in shock at what he saw.

Severed from his body, the head of George Fangman hung suspended by a wire from the overhanging branch. The assassin's hemorrhaging, blood-veined eyes stared wide open, directly at Peppe Palmisano. Blood dripped on the terrace.

Peppe screamed in pure animal terror, gagging and vomiting. Lupe dropped her tray of coffee. She burst out sobbing. Palmisano's bodyguards drew their weapons but didn't know whom to shoot. Lupe had the presence of mind to telephone Palmisano's personal physician, but by the time the doctor arrived, Peppe had regained his senses.

A flicker of pure fear appeared in Peppe's eyes. How, he wondered, could anyone have penetrated his tightly secured compound? The men on night duty claimed that they had heard nothing. To Peppe, this seemed incomprehensible. Were his own Mafia people conspiring against him? Whoever killed Fangman had power, cunning and ruthlessness that exceeded anything Palmisano had ever experienced. Peppe had the reputation of not being a stupid man; just a supremely egotistical one.

Palmisano felt his chest tighten. If word of the "head-on-the-tree" ever got out, the Tampa mob boss would lose face within the Casa Nostra and be laughed at by Zúñiga's Colombians. That decided him. Peppe gave the necessary orders. His bodyguards swung into action. They buried Fangman's head in a secret place on the estate. Six hours later, Peppe traveled in an armored car to the Tampa airport for his 12:15 one-way Alitalia flight to Rome via Atlanta and from there to Palermo, Sicily for an extended visit.

"SENOR ZÚÑIGA, IS LUPE," Peppe Palmisano's maid mumbled on the cell phone in a choking whisper. "You pay me good. You tell me call you." She started to cry. "Oh my God, in my whole life I never see—"

"Speak, woman," Zúñiga demanded.

"I bring to Don Peppe his coffee on terrace. He go to pick his peach and—"

Zúñiga heard the sound of gagging. "And what?"

"God forgive me," Lupe stammered. "The head—like Saint John the Baptist."

"Someone cut off Don Peppe's head?" Zúñiga roared.

"No. Not Senor Palmisano's. He leave. He go back Sicily."

"Whose head was it?"

"Don Peppe's bodyguards, they no say."

Cezar Zúñiga hung up. He speed dialed on a secure line that rang 550 miles away in Cartegena, Colombia.

"Miguel," Zúñiga ordered. "Contact *La Carcharodon.* I have a contract for him in Florida. I am giving a gift to a friend—a Colombian necktie. I want Angel to cut the gringo's throat and pull his tongue out through the slit. Then murder his family."

...33

"THE WAR IS ON," Nurkiewicz announced with veiled excitement. He focused on the fax in front of him. Fernandez, Manion and Latisha Du Burns listened as Nurkiewicz said, "Our Tampa office reports the Palmisano mob is circling the wagons. At 12:15 A.M. yesterday, Peppe Palmisano boarded an Alitalia flight to Rome. Peppe's crew is milling around the Palmisano compound. It looks like they're going to the mattresses."

Fernandez looked troubled. "Why the sudden crisis?"

"It should be obvious," Nurkiewicz shot back. "Palmisano felt threatened by Wolffe and let out a contract. Not unexpected. Police found fingerprints on a stolen van in Tampa and ran them through our IAF identification system. The prints belong to an old Mafia hitman named George Fangman. The Trenton police checked with Fangman's family. His wife's worried. She claimed that George left on a consulting job in Florida and had not returned home or contacted her, which she claims is highly unusual." He paused and grinned. "I believe this means Georgie boy isn't ever coming home. My guess is that Palmisano found out his hired gun got clipped and he panicked. Now blood is going to flow."

Manion, too, looked unconvinced. "From what I've heard, George Fangman ranked at the top of his profession; a cold, disciplined and lethal son of a bitch."

"Aren't we jumping the gun a little?" Fernandez asked. "I can't believe this Wolffe, or whatever his real name is—"

Nurkiewicz broke in, red-faced. "I don't give a rat's ass what you believe." He spoke slowly, with barely suppressed anger at being challenged. "You people don't belong—"

Nurkiewicz looked at Latisha, caught himself, and stopped. He nodded to Manion. Both men got up and left.

"THAT MAN IS A PIECE OF WORK. Why do you put up with him?" Latisha scowled.

Fernandez didn't know the answer.

She arched her eyebrows. "I watched *The Sopranos*, but I never believed people could just fork over money and purchase a contract killer as easy as buying a refrigerator. How many of these badasses are around?"

"Nobody knows. There is no census taken. Maybe a hundred, if you count the semi-retired and novices who have the knack. Some years ago, the FBI listed the world's four most notorious. Ilich Ramírez Sánchez is a Venezuelan known as 'Carlos the Jackal.' He is now serving a life sentence in a French prison.

"Second is the Israeli, Uri Rechmann, known as 'Shivaman.' Rechmann was a member of the Mossad hit team that revenged the murders of the Israeli Olympic athletes at Munich. Then Rechmann went rogue, operating as a hired assassin in Europe and the Middle East. He died in an explosion in Afghanistan six or seven years ago. Good riddance.

"Third is the American hitman, Richard 'The Iceman' Kuklinski, one of the most diabolical self-confessed contract killers in American history. He took credit for over 200 murders. Kuklinski died in a New Jersey prison in 2006. George Fangman was the protégé of Kuklinski."

He paused. "The last is an albino Colombian named Angel Aguilera. Aguilera only operated in South America, so we don't know whether he is still alive. They called him *La Carcharodon*, the 'White Shark.' "

...34

ANGEL AGUILERA was a short albino man. He wore extra clothing and a large floppy hat to protect his skin from the blazing noonday Florida sun. His congenital disorder was caused by a defective hereditary enzyme, resulting in a partial absence of pigment in skin, hair and eyes. Angel had platinum-white hair and reddish-pink eyes, a little hooded behind dark protective goggles. Being short-sighted, his gaze constantly wandered as he moved the vibrating leaf blower slowly in fluid motion. In Florida, nobody paid leaf blowers any mind. They were like palm trees, a natural part of the landscape.

As a favor to Cezar Zúñiga, a local landscaping company owner had arranged for Angel Aguilera to be included in the crew of unregistered Mexican immigrants raking, pruning shrubs and trimming trees in Ocean Village.

Aguilera checked the address provided by his handler. The Wolffes' house nested on a corner lot not far from the beach. After murdering the family, Angel's instructions were to proceed south along the beach 200 yards to where a motorcycle had been hidden and then head north on A1A, crossing the Indian River at the Fort Pierce Inlet before the bridge could be blocked off by police.

He checked his watch: 1:30 P.M. Angel touched the loop of wire in the back of his waistband. The garrote always proved to be fast, silent and effective. No one in South America could whip it around a victim's neck faster than the White Shark.

Angel Aguilera wiped a sheen of sweat from his forehead. He cautiously approached the back patio door, looking around before knocking. In the ninety-four-degree heat, there was no one in sight. The door opened before he had a chance to ring the bell. An elderly white-haired lady eyed him up and down with an inquisitive smile.

"You're the man Barry sent to fix my screens?"

Angel answered in an indecipherable grunt.

"I wasn't expecting you until this afternoon. Good, now I can go shopping."

Angel closed his eyes and took in a deep breath, inhaling the familiar whiff of chicken *sancoho*, mingled with the aroma of sausage and garlic.

Rosalie led him on to the porch. "The tiny no-see-ums and mosquitoes are driving me crazy. I can't stand it anymore. Do you need a screwdriver or stepladder?"

Angel nodded with feigned enthusiasm, studying the screens. "Wheels is stuck." He stood on the stepladder and made a half turn with the screwdriver. Then he got down on his knees and adjusted the bottom wheels.

"You got *lubricante*?"

Rosalie fetched a can of aluminum lubricant, and Angel sprayed the tracks, opening and closing the screens to insure they operated smoothly. He smiled. "Is okay?"

"You are wonderful. What is your name?"

"Angel."

"Angel, would you like a beer?"

He accepted the bottle with a nod of thanks. The woman facing him reminded him of his mother in Aguachica, the small village in the southern region of the Cesar Department. The same gray hair, the plump frame. It had been so long that he couldn't conjure up a picture of his mother's face. It had almost faded from his memory. He regarded her in silence.

"You look hungry. Sit. Sit. You taste my cooking. Yes?"

Angel perched on a stool at the table. He could feel the loop of wire resting against his lumbar spine. Parched, he finished the beer and tasted the chicken.

"Is good; same like my mother's."

Rosalie opened another Heineken for Angel and poured one for herself. "When did you last see your mother?"

Aguilera's eyed narrowed. "Long time."

"Do you miss her... your mama?"

At first Aguilera didn't respond. He took a long gulp. After a moment, he nodded slowly.

A tear appeared in the corner of Rosalie's eye. "I could never have children, but if I had a fine son like you, it would kill me to be separated." She finished off her beer. "Time moves on, and before you know it, the people we love are gone... forever."

There was an awkward pause. "Go see your mother before it is too late. She named you her Angel. She loves you."

"I don't know."

"Do you need to borrow money for the trip to Colombia?"

"No. I have work."

She put a gentle hand on his shoulder. "Could you forgive yourself if your mother died and you were too busy fixing screens for Barry to go to her? Could you, Angel? Could you?"

Angel Aguilera made a sudden decision. The albino killer hugged Rosalie in his arms, kissing her on both cheeks. "*Gracias. Gracias*," he whispered.

"Angel. You forgot your leaf blower," she yelled after him.

"WHY HAVEN'T I BEEN INFORMED?" Cesar Zúñiga demanded. His voice carried a threatening note. "It has been 24 hours. Is the job done?"

"I'm sorry, Señor Zúñiga," the voice on the phone answered. "Angel does not answer his cell. He did not pick up his money, and he never returned to his motel." Zúñiga heard a deep sigh. "I fear *La Carcharodon esta muerto*."

ROSALIE RETURNED FROM THE HAIRDRESSER'S. She entered the kitchen, rinsed off the dishes and stacked them randomly in the dishwasher. Her doorbell rang. Two police officers stood in the doorway, one a heavyset African-American woman, the other a big man, broad-shouldered, over fifty, with tired eyes and a grim smile, wearing a suit and tie. Rosalie stared at the pair. Her face stiffened.

"Mrs. Wolffe?" the woman asked. "May we come in?"

Rosalie's pulse quickened. "What's wrong?"

"Ma'am, I am Sergeant Vesta Jones from the Fort Pierce Police. This is Detective Carlson. We regret to inform you of the death of your brother, Bernard Rothstein."

Rosalie stared at the sergeant and shook her head. "Bernie," she gasped, slumping down in a chair. Tears welled in her eyes. Sergeant Jones handed her a tissue.

"I knew it would happen. Bernie had a history of heart trouble. He never took care of himself. He ate all that fried—"

"No, ma'am," Detective Carlson broke in gently. "Mr. Bernard Rothstein was murdered."

...36

"BERNIE THE ATTORNEY" ROTHSTEIN was buried in Riverview Memorial Park in Fort Pierce. A small gathering attended the graveside service. A young rabbi from Port St. Lucie officiated. The rabbi, a tall, long-limbed, gawky, red-haired fellow, wore a gray suit with no tie. He reminded Big Mike De Luca of a sandhill crane. The rabbi spoke at length about the good traits of the deceased man he had never met.

"At this moment we are about to lay Bernard Rothstein's body to rest. This is not the moment to shed tears; rather we should be thankful we were given the chance to have known a decent man named Bernard Rothstein and how much he touched our lives."

Eddie Rizzo took his turn shoveling dirt over the lowered casket. He whispered to Crazy Sal Scarlotti, "If Bernie hadn't touched my life, I would still be serving ten to fifteen in the Illinois super-max."

Battaglia put down his cane, took the shovel from Rizzo and tossed dirt. Turning to De Luca, he grinned. "Putting people in the ground is like old times for you, eh, Mike?"

"If what that rabbi said was true," De Luca muttered, "it ain't Bernie in this here box."

ONE HOUR LATER, the funeral attendees gathered at the Wolffes' home. Standing on the patio, Crazy Sal Scarlotti slurped a beer and waved a mosquito out of his face. "Fuckin' bugs will drive you crazy." He added, "I owed Bernie big time. He made me keep my mouth shut—tight. He told me, 'No bodies, no victims, no problems.' "

95

After his fourth beer, Scarlotti asked, "Was it you who done Hoffa, Mike?" De Luca offered a dour smile, shrugged and reached for another corned beef sandwich.

Sergeant Vesta Jones felt herself tense up as she prepared to pay her respects to the family. "You have my sincere condolences for your loss, ma'am."

Rosalie tried a feeble smile. She wearily rubbed her red eyes. "I have to make more coffee."

Wolffe gave her a curious glance. "How did Bernard die?"

"A patrol car discovered Mr. Rothstein's body while making rounds. At first, the police thought he was sleeping, but a white man asleep in a Cadillac in the Lincoln Park area at 5 A.M. is very unusual. According to the medical examiner, your brother-in-law received two shots in the head—at close range."

Wolffe remained silent.

"I saw the crime scene photos. The old man's clothes were soaked with blood. Whoever killed him tied a red bandana around his neck as some kind of a sick joke."

"Have you arrested anyone?"

"No. People might know who did the killing, but because of fear or apathy, nobody talks. People have friends or family in the area and are afraid to testify. The red bandana tells us that Mr. Rothstein's killer most likely belonged to a gang called the Bloods. But, unfortunately, we can't prove a case with no physical evidence and no witnesses—just a nice old dead man and shell casings on the ground."

"Did Bernie have a relationship with the Bloods?"

"At our last meeting at the stationhouse, I explained the gangs. Like I told the guys, in Fort Pierce, the Bloods wear red shirts, caps and bandanas, and the Crips wear blue. We estimate the Bloods to have over one hundred members. These guys are well organized and are responsible for most of the drugs and murders in town. Mr.

Rothstein talked about mediating with the Crips and Bloods, maybe arranging a sit-down."

"Sounds like Bernard."

"I know those old guys bent the rules, and I cut them some slack, but I warned them as clearly as I could not to be messin' with the gangs."

Vesta Jones added, "Mr. Rothstein told me everybody wanted something, that the art of negotiation was finding out what it was each side wanted most and then reconciling the differences. Off the record, I think that old man personally tried to negotiate a meeting between the Bloods and the Crips."

"And how did Bernie know who to mediate with?"

"I'm afraid that it is not possible to share that information."

Wolffe spoke softly in a dangerous kind of way. "Sergeant, Bernard Rothstein died doing *your* job. I want the names of the gang leaders. And I want them *now*."

Vesta saw his eyes. Behind them, she saw only darkness. In her entire life she had never felt so frightened. A change had come over Mr. Wolffe.

As she explained it to her life partner that evening, he suddenly seemed different, scary—and she decided she'd better answer the man. It was years before Vesta Jones could put it out of her mind.

Police Probe Double Shooting

FORT PIERCE—Fort Pierce police are investigating a double murder in the 700 block of North 20th Street that occurred at approximately 4 A.M. yesterday morning. Two victims have been identified as Jermorey Williams and Devonte Clark. Both men were shot in the center of their foreheads—execution style. Williams is believed to be the gang leader of a group called the Bloods, and Clark the head of a rival gang, the Crips.

Inside the house, investigators seized a quantity of cocaine and marijuana, sandwich bags, a digital scale, and a dozen weapons including assault rifles, handguns and shotguns. Police Chief Jerry Sollins commented, "There are a lot of questions we can't answer, and a lot of questions we won't be able to answer until we get further into the investigation.

"This was not a random act," Sollins added. "These victims were targeted. Williams' body had a red bandana tied around his neck, and Devonte Clark's had a blue one."

...38

"OLD MACKY'S BACK IN TOWN." Charlie Manion winked at Fernandez. He handed Latisha a disk. "Make yourself useful, honey. Slip this in your laptop. The tech boys monitoring our wiretap on Marcus Wolffe came up with this audio gem. They thought the conversation sounded suspicious and converted the words of both parties into bits of data and matched it against another database of preloaded voiceprints."

Fernandez looked puzzled.

"Increase the volume," Manion requested as Latisha clicked on the disc.

"Mr. Wolffe?"

"Yes."

"I am a business associate of Don Peppe Palmisano. His organization handles the sales and the distribution of my company's products in Florida."

No response.

"Unfortunately, Don Peppe has taken an extended vacation in Europe, and as such, he will not be able to provide my product line the attention it requires."

"Do I know you?"

"Walls have big ears. Please call me Cesar. I understand that you are expanding your business, and I believe that we share mutual interests. In view of the Tampa situation, we will be revising our sales representation in Florida. I would appreciate the opportunity to meet personally to discuss the competitive advantages of my merchandise."

"Why did you contact me?"

"An angel left a message that I could not ignore."

"I don't know what you're talking about."

*"Come, sir. No false modesty. I am aware of your recent ac-
complishment, settling a problem, dare I say, peachfully."*

"You've got the wrong party."

"Think it over, Mr.—"

The sound of a call disconnected.

FERNANDEZ' PULSE RACED; his temples throbbed. "Is
that who I think it is?"

Manion nodded. "Your old buddy, Cezar Zúñiga."

A chill went through Fernandez hearing Zúñiga's name; the
man responsible for his failed Miami operation, responsible for his
FBI career being short-circuited; the man who had arranged for the
sniper to fire two bullets into his chest. Fernandez was trained to
appear impassive, but now his heart thudded so hard that he wasn't
aware of the iPhone vibrating in his pocket.

Latisha watched his face turn ashen as he answered it. She
saw puzzlement, concern and then fear.

"But Uri Rechmann is dead," he mumbled into the phone.

"Interpol's in a tizzy," Darlene replied. "It's a dead-on photo
match, Frank."

"Darlene, I need a huge favor. Keep this off the Bureau's
radar for 48 hours." Then he disconnected.

"Uri Rechmann's alive," Manion blurted out. "Shivaman
himself. No shit? You better tell Nurkiewicz."

"Nurkiewicz is a loose cannon. He'll go apeshit. It's his big
chance for promotion and the Meritorious Achievement medal. I
need time to sort things out."

"Cut the crap, *amigo*. I'm not risking my career for you."

Anger and frustration flooded Fernandez. He lunged forward. With both hands he grabbed Manion by the front of his shirt,

slamming him against the wall. He pressed a hard elbow against the man's throat, choking him. Fernandez spoke in a low, dark voice full of rage. "I've put up with your shit long enough. If you breathe one word, I'll goddamn kill you."

Manion's face flushed purple, his eyes widened in shock. He brought his hands up to free himself, but Fernandez maintained the pressure until Manion nodded and slumped into a chair, gasping for air in his lungs.

Fernandez glanced at his watch: 2:00. He hit his iPhone contact list. "This is Agent Frank Fernandez. I need to see the director immediately." He waited. "No. Tomorrow's not an option. Tell him I'm on my way to his office." He hung up.

...39

FERNANDEZ PACED IMPATIENTLY outside Glenner's office, thinking about Cesar Zúñiga and the warehouse shooting. Was he chasing old ghosts in a futile, endless hope of redemption for the failed Miami operation? Maybe he had become simply a burnt-out agent, and these delusions were symptoms that it was time to go. But his gut told him differently.

Fernandez knew that he was flawed in many ways. His ex-wife could testify to that. But he wasn't a hypocrite. He had sworn to uphold the law as he believed it to be, and that was why he had to talk to his friend. Both had served with the 1st Battalion, 5th Marine Regiment, one of the first Marine ground combat units in Iraq during the start of Operation Iraqi Freedom in 2003. Captain William Glenner had been Fernandez' company commander.

"WHAT'S THE PANIC, FRANK?" William Glenner asked. "Close the door. Sit down. You look like hell." Glenner looked to be in his mid-fifties, with hazel green eyes, an angular face and strong jaw. His curly brown hair was flecked with gray.

The early-afternoon sun filtered through two polarized glass windows equipped with piezoelectric oscillators, rendering futile any attempts at laser-acoustic surveillance from outside. The FBI director's office was large, clean and sparsely furnished with high-end modern furniture. The walls were painted a muted gray. A slab of black granite topped Glenner's desk. On the wall behind the desk hung a portrait of the President. A furled Stars and Stripes stood like sentinel in a corner.

Fernandez took a seat in front of him. "Have you heard the parable of the blind men and the elephant?"

Glenner shook his head and glanced at his watch. "Is this going to take long?"

Fernandez shrugged that off. "Four blind men in India were trying to comprehend an elephant. One man touched a side of the elephant. He thought it was a wall. Another leaned on the tusk and believed it to be a spear. The third man touched the trunk, certain it was a snake. The fourth man felt a knee, knowing it was a tree."

He could see Glenner's eyes wandering.

"The point of my story, Bill, is that I feel like a blind man trying to understand a scary, giant elephant. I can touch it in several different spots, but I can't connect the dots and get to the truth."

"What does Nurk say?"

"I haven't told him yet. I will, though."

Glenner looked over his glasses. "You haven't told your superior officer?"

"The guy is a loose cannon. He's afraid you'll reduce his fiefdom and reallocate resources to counter-terrorism."

The director spread his hands on the granite desk, as if bracing himself for the unpleasant job he had to do. "Frank, I was the best man at your wedding. We served together in the Corps. In many ways, you're like a brother. I run a bureau with 535 members of Congress looking over my shoulders. I not only report to Congress, but also to the attorney general and the President. This job is under constant media attention. Every e-mail, every memorandum, every little secret is in constant danger of being leaked or written about in an autobiography. And then I give my people weapons and send them out to do dangerous work that impacts directly on our nation's safety."

After being silent for a moment, his eyes settled on his friend. Then in a gentle, pained voice he continued, "As important to me as loyalty is, to most of the people in this building, it's cold-hearted pragmatism that rules the day. You know that."

He continued, speaking evenly. "You are a good FBI agent, Frank. Persistent." He winked. "And occasionally astute. You know I can't get involved in the middle of a Bureau personnel problem. Noses are still out of joint over Waco. You ignored channels, and I covered for you. Then after you got out of the hospital, I interceded to keep you on active duty. Maybe it's time—"

Fernandez interrupted. Opening a folder, he slid out an 8 x 10 color print. "Do you recognize this man?"

"Looks like that son-of-a-bitch Lindsay from the CIA."

"How about the person he's chatting up?"

"No. Who is he?"

"Does the name Uri Rechmann sound familiar?"

The FBI director's eyes narrowed. He studied the picture more closely. "Where and when was this taken?" Glenner snapped.

"Last week. In Florida."

"Rechmann is alive and here in this country? Jesus Christ." He grabbed the phone. "Amy, cancel all my appointments today." He hesitated. "Tell the attorney general that I have the flu. And two coffees, please—black."

He turned to Fernandez. "Start over. And I don't want to hear about elephant dung. Tell me something real, something *concrete*."

Fernandez started from the beginning and explained everything. He concluded by saying, "I told Nurkiewicz that if I hadn't heard that restaurant tape myself, I would never have connected Rechmann to the Mafia. It didn't compute. Wolffe had no previous police record, not even a traffic violation. Why would the world's number one assassin come out of hiding and expose himself to publicity? Nurk wouldn't listen. He believed Wolffe to be planning a takeover in Florida and there would be a gang war."

"Yes. He told me that."

Fernandez continued. "Then Nurkiewicz obsessed about a group of old men who probably moved to Florida for the warm weather." He took a deep breath. "I do have to give Nurk credit for his professional paranoia. He ordered wire taps on Wolffe's phone and photos to be taken of everything the man did. On this point, he was right.

"When I recognized the CIA's Black Ops boss in the photograph on the beach, I hand-carried Wolffe's picture to Justice and had a friend forward it to Interpol. I had no inkling of his identity. If I had told Nurkiewicz, he would have exploded like a bull in a china shop. This Rechmann business must be sorted out rationally. There are too many serious implications."

Glenner nodded in agreement.

"There's more."

"You're giving me a headache."

"Welcome to the elephant, Bill. Just when I'm trying to make sense of the trunk, the tusk and the knee, I touch more confusing parts. I hate to admit it, but Nurkiewicz might have been right all along about a Mafia showdown. Two days ago a hitman named George Fangman was reported missing by his wife in New Jersey. He had gone to Tampa on a job."

Fernandez paused to sip coffee. "Fangman never returned home. Yesterday, the Tampa police received reports that the Palmisano crime family is gathering at the boss's estate. They may be 'going to the mattresses.' "

He took a deep breath. "And wait till you hear this. The phone tap Nurkiewicz ordered on Rechmann's phone picked up a call from a person who has been positively voice identified as... Cesar Zúñiga."

Glenner sat back, grimacing. "I'm not hearing answers, Frank. I remember Zúñiga. That's old news. In this business we all have setbacks, then we pick up the pieces and move on. You have never moved on. Maybe if I had had two 7.62 millimeter bullets drilled into my chest, I would have acted the same way."

The director continued, "Listen to me, man. I'm speaking as your boss and your friend. This *elephant* of yours is too big for you to try and handle alone: Rechmann alive and operating in the United States; CIA Black Ops involvement; a potential Mafia war. I'm going to form a special task force to deal with these issues. I want you to—"

Fernandez held up both hands. "Do what you have to do, Bill. But, as a friend, please grant me one favor first."

"What?" Glenner asked dryly.

"I want to meet with Rechmann. He has no outstanding warrants in the U.S.—"

"Goddamn it, Frank, what are you thinking?" Glenner broke in. "You are not in good physical shape, and you want to sit down with an international assassin and have a nice chat? Am I missing something?"

"Give me 24 hours."

"Let's put this argument out of its misery. I will not, I repeat *not*, under any circumstances, grant your request. This isn't the Marines anymore." Glenner stood up. "And you're not John fucking Wayne."

PART II

...40

AT DAWN FERNANDEZ GOT UP, brewed coffee and ordered a cab to take him to Ronald Reagan National Airport. Waiting for the 10:30 A.M. U.S. Airways flight to Palm Beach, he took a seat in the waiting area, opened his briefcase and started studying Rechmann's dossier that had been telexed to the FBI by Interpol.

> Skeletal History: International criminal (assassin) Uri Rechmann. Born Jerusalem, Israel 1937. Rechmann is also known as *Shivaman*. The meaning is uncertain, possibly taken from the Hindu three-eyed god known as Lord Shiva the destroyer. Shiva is many times depicted as of dark complexion and at other times is considered as white as camphor. Lord Shiva's anger is believed to instill fear in all beings, and his third eye opens only to punish wrong doers.

When he boarded his flight, Fernandez took his assigned window seat, buckled himself in, and continued reading. The A320 single aisle jetliner swung into line, paused, trembled and then hurled itself down the runway. The nose lifted, the rear wheels lost contact, the ground below tilted forty-five degrees, and Washington dropped quickly away. He was so absorbed in his reading, he hardly noticed.

> Raised in Israel, Uri Rechmann enlisted in the *Kidon*, the assassination unit of Mossad. For Mossad to order assassinations was a very formalized procedure requiring the Prime Minister to sign off and initial each name on any assassination list, or it could not be carried out. People in Mossad and Shin Bet had been forced out for ordering killings

without approval from the top. Under these circumstances Rechmann separated from the Israeli military service.

The natural areas in which former military experts sought lucrative employment were bodyguard work, industrial counterespionage, security consultation, and for a specially trained few, assassinations. Rechmann parlayed his skills and language fluency into a livelihood.

Sometime after 1970, Interpol listed Rechmann as an international criminal. Over the years, few details surfaced about the man—only fragmentary bits of evidence ever identified individuals or nationalities that employed him.

DEPARTING PALM BEACH AIRPORT, Fernandez took the I-95 ramp north towards Fort Pierce. He stuffed the Rechmann dossier into his attaché case for further reading. Reactivating his iPhone, he noted three messages received while in flight.

"Frank, Bill Glenner here. Sorry if I overreacted, pal. I'm worried about you. Maybe you returned to active status too soon. I think you should see someone professionally. There's a doctor at the VA Medical Center who has had good results working with post-traumatic stress veterans. Give Dr. Russo a buzz at 202-745-7577. She will be expecting your call."

"Frank. This is Latisha. Mr. N. knows about 'you-know-who,' and it wasn't me who told him. He's running around like a chicken with his head cut off trying to reach you."

"Fernandez. Nurkiewicz here. Call before I can your ass!"

Fernandez understood that his actions were impulsive, potentially career ending—even dangerous. He followed his GPS route guide from I-95 to Monterey Road, then right on Seaway Drive over two bridges to A1A. Heading north, he could see the Atlantic on his right. Heat lightning flickered silently along the eastern horizon.

His iPhone chimed. It was Nurkiewicz again. Fernandez let it ring. His thoughts raced, thinking about the Interpol report. The image of the dead man pictured in the newspaper *Novaya Gazetas* still lodged in Fernandez' mind: blood coagulating down the front of the victim's forehead and shirtfront like a necktie. He didn't want to underestimate Rechmann. The old operative had the reputation of a killing machine.

At the Ocean Village guard gate, Fernandez smiled and flashed his FBI badge. The small guard with alert eyes asked, "May I ask the nature of your visit, sir?"

"If I told you, I'd have to kill you."

The guard laughed at the old joke. He winked, saluted and raised the bar.

Fernandez felt his stomach tighten as he turned right on Windward Drive, checked the address and pulled up to the one-story, tan stucco structure with orange clay tiles on the roof. Two grayish-brown coconut palm trees guarded the front entrance.

Breathing shallowly, he rang the front doorbell. No sounds emanated from inside. He felt a prickle in his neck, a creepy feeling. In the graying light, the swaying coconut palms cast eerie shadows. Something flickered in his peripheral vision. A vein pulsed in Fernandez' temple. He felt the needle tip of a knife just below the lobe of his right ear and froze. Without a sound, someone materialized behind him. A low, accented voice whispered in his ear, "Weapon, wallet and phone, please."

"TASTE THE HONEY," said Uri Rechmann quietly. "One tablespoon per pitcher. It releases the natural sweetness of iced tea."

Fernandez felt suddenly and unpleasantly short of breath. He was determined not to show it. He studied the man dressed in dark trousers, an open white sport shirt and sneakers on bare feet. Fernandez looked at Rechmann's dark, craggy face and noticed how his hands shook with a slight tremor as he added the honey. Age at least seventy-five, Fernandez supposed. The legendary assassin's eyes were neutral, guarded, his features lined and worn. A casual observer might think the man to be courteous and kindly, even harmless, not an internationally feared killer.

Rechmann cradled Fernandez' iPhone. He replayed the three messages. "This man, Glenner, is your FBI director?"

Fernandez nodded.

"Also your *pal*?"

"We served together in the Marines."

"You served together, yet he is the director and you are still only a special agent?"

"I can explain—"

Rechmann gave a dismissive wave. "And the girl—"

"A summer intern."

With the circumspection that comes naturally to men of the clandestine profession, Rechmann's voice turned steely. "Were these calls choreographed for my benefit?" Without waiting for a reply, Rechmann touched Latisha's voicemail icon.

"Is that you, Frank?" a nervous voice answered.

"Agent Fernandez requested I call you, ma'am," Rechmann improvised. "He wished for you to know that he is fine—"

Latisha cut him off sharply. "You tell that low-life that if he left town without saying goodbye, I am seriously pissed." She took a breath. "And also tell him that the goddamned icicle is melting away." She hung up.

"The lady is annoyed. She wished you to know about an icicle. Is it a code?"

For the first time, Fernandez laughed. "I told her when she joined the Bureau that trust was like an icicle: once it melts, that's the end of it."

Rechmann shrugged. "The only people I trust to do me no harm are corpses." He put down his mug of tea. "Now young man, foreplay is over." His eyes bored into Fernandez. "You have no monitoring device taped to your chest. You say that you know who I am. You are an FBI agent, but you do not arrive with your cavalry. Why?"

"It's a long story—"

Rechmann interrupted. "The abbreviated version, please. How did your FBI learn of my identity? I have nothing to fear from international authorities. But after years in this business, you make enemies. No matter what precautions one takes, if they really want to find you—they will. That is the unwritten certainty of the profession. So. How did you uncover me?"

Fernandez spoke calmly, explaining everything.

Rechmann shook his head sadly. "Careless of me not to check for a tap on my telephone."

"What do you mean that you have nothing to fear from international authorities? I understand that Interpol went bananas."

"Later. I need to know what your people are planning." He handed back the phone. "Find out."

Fernandez called Latisha. His speakerphone was on.

"Yeah?" Latisha answered, her voice hollow. "Is it you this time, or your flunky with the fake accent?"

"Latisha, calm down, please. I will explain everything. Is Nurkiewicz planning an operation in Fort Pierce? I need to know."

"The man's in and out of Glenner's office like a revolving door. They're waiting for a go-ahead from Interpol."

"Thank you, Latisha. I'll call you back."

Rechmann raised a questioning eyebrow. "How is a young girl privy to such information?"

"Her father is a Congressman, chairman of the House committee that monitors FBI appropriations."

"Excuse me for a moment," Rechmann said. "Old men's bladder problem."

Once inside the house, Rechmann punched in a rarely used number on his secure encrypted phone.

"Yes?

"A sterile line?"

"Of course."

"The FBI knows my identity and location."

"Have they been in touch?"

"Indirectly."

"Extraterritoriality?"

"They are waiting for Interpol."

"Timing?"

"Indeterminate."

"Let me make a few calls. Prepare to disappear again, my friend."

"No. I'm tired of running,"

...41

AN HOUR LATER, a high haze crept over the darkening sky. Uri Rechmann hunched forward in his chair. "Why are you really here, Agent Fernandez: patriotism, ambition or revenge? If it were ambition, you would not have come alone for fear I could terminate your life."

Fernandez remained silent.

"Patriotism I doubt, as there are no open warrants for my arrest in the United States. That leaves revenge. If your motive is revenge..." Rechmann smiled. "It cannot involve me. There is no hate in your eyes. Interesting. So it must have to do with this fellow on the telephone call, Zúñiga. Yes?"

Fernandez nodded. "Zúñiga is a major narco-trafficker. I was wounded attempting to execute a federal arrest warrant on the man. Our plans were leaked. I got shot twice in the chest."

"Lift up your shirt."

Rechmann peered at the twin welts of pinkish scar tissue. His brows creased. "What caliber bullets?"

"They were 7.62 millimeter, fired from about a hundred yards away."

Rechmann nodded. "Subsonic ammunition. With that caliber it had to be a Vaime Mk 2 silenced sniper rifle. Were the bullets removed?"

"Not all. Too many fragments."

"How long ago?"

"Two years."

Rechmann scowled. "Your wound is not healing as it should. When you get back to Washington, see a doctor." Without further comment, the Israeli walked to a cluster of dark-colored flowers. "My hobby is cultivating daylilies. This three-eyed tetraploid is my favorite, a little hard to see at dusk. Notice the emerald blood red throat and the six-inch purplish-black petals."

Fernandez' phone chimed.

Nurkiewicz brayed into the phone, "Is that you, you insubordinate son-of-a-bitch? I expect you in my office no later than nine o'clock tomorrow morning, and I don't care if you have to charter a private jet to get here. Your arrogance is amazing. You're finished, Fernandez."

After a few seconds he realized Nurkiewicz had hung up. He inhaled slowly, struggling to tamp down his anger.

Rechmann went into the house, returning with two filled glasses. "Do you know why Jews say *l'chaim* when they drink wine?"

Fernandez slapped at a mosquito and shook his head.

"Two reasons: at one time they used to give wine to the condemned, so that their executions would be less painful."

"Are you preparing to have me eaten alive by mosquitoes?"

Rechmann ignored his attempt at humor. "The plural of *l'chaim* is translated as 'two lives,' meaning that no one should live life alone. We all need someone else."

Fernandez thought of Latisha and his growing attachment to the girl. It was increasing the more time he spent with her. "I'll drink to that. Hell, I'm getting fired, I'll drink to anything."

"Stop wallowing in self-pity. For you to confront me alone took a brave man or a fool. You don't strike me as a fool, and my survival instincts are well honed. You may lose your job, but not your life. Go find a good woman and a new job."

They settled into another silence, less tense and more companionable. Darkness had settled. He could hear the rhythm of the waves breaking on shore a block away. Fernandez' mind swirled with questions.

"How do you know Alex Lindsay?"

"What will you give me in return?"

Fernandez wasn't sure he had anything a man of Rechmann's reach would want. "How about information?"

"About what?"

"Anything you want. If I know it, I'll answer the question."

The Israeli smiled. "I like your style." Rechmann remained silent for a moment. "Alex Lindsay and I are acquaintances. When adversaries are not at each other's throats, people in our business chat if they can. You learn things that can be useful later on."

He was lying, Fernandez knew. "When I mentioned Interpol and asked what you meant about having nothing to fear from international authorities, you told me, 'later.' "

In a flat voice, Rechmann answered, "I became an equal opportunity employee."

"You worked for the CIA?"

"Once or twice a year—it paid me well. And the Europeans did as well—that is why Interpol is caught in their underwear. They know I have secrets that everyone would prefer remain buried. These are my insurance policies. One set of copies is deposited with a lawyer in Israel whom I know to be trustworthy, and another set of copies is sealed in a safe-deposit box, insulated and protected. These officials do not want me dead, nor do they wish for me to be around. They want me in limbo."

"After the plane crash, you went to Johns Hopkins to change your appearance?"

"Being in the hospital with serious facial nerve damage was a cathartic experience. I decided I no longer had the patience for protracted flight. It was time that I was out of the *game*. I wanted to be left in peace. But I knew there never would be any peace."

"If you valued your... peace, why on earth did you become a Mafia capo? I could never understand that."

Rechmann's eyes widened. "Mafia. Are you insane?"

"I saw you enter the Baltimore Italian restaurant."

He frowned. "My wife wanted us to be godparents for her masseuse's kid. Like a foolish husband, I agreed."

"Why did you move from Baltimore to Fort Pierce?"

"Isn't it everyone's dream to retire to a warm climate and spend the rest of your years in the sun? As an Israeli, I missed the sea." He sighed. "The truth is, geography solves nothing."

"What about your Orange Blossom mob?"

"Who?"

"The old Mafiosos."

"Those men were friends of my brother-in-law, Bernard. I met them at the funeral for the first time. What did you call them?"

"Never mind. How you got the name *Shiva?*"

"The truth is a disappointment. Someone in the Israeli Mossad first assigned it to me as my code name. They called me *Shivah-maker*, or as you Americans might say, *Widow-maker*. The word Shivah means seven. It is the weeklong Jewish mourning for close relatives."

In the darkness Rechmann disappeared, then returned holding a daylily. "I named this 'Lord Shiva.' Would you like to know why?" Without waiting, he answered his question. "Lord Shiva is the destroyer, the most powerful god of the Hindu pantheon. Shiva is depicted as having three eyes: the sun is his right eye, the moon the left eye, and fire is the center eye.

"In this age of lightning-fast communications, the name Shiva reverberated in the press. I suppose that, after the Jackal, the media needed a new name to provoke fear and... readership. I should be pleased that they didn't choose another animal's name."

"Did you kill George Fangman?" Fernandez broke in.

"No more questions. Go home."

"One last one. Why would an international fugitive get married and make himself—so to speak—a hostage to fortune?"

Rechmann raised his eyes to the ceiling and exhaled. "I wish I knew that answer." He lifted his wine glass. *"L'chaim."*

...42

"INTERPOL is consulting with its European counterparts," Manion explained. "They're discussing whether to send an incident response team, or formally request the FBI to handle Rechmann's capture and extradition. Word from the Justice department is that they expect Interpol to get around to it by sometime next week."

A short bark of derision from Nurkiewicz. "Great sense of urgency. As soon as we get the green light, I want to be able to strike quickly."

"Should I alert state and local law enforcement agencies?"

"No way. I want no leaks," Nurkiewicz groused. "We'll brief those people at the very last minute to avoid what happened on the Miami raid. What is our force status?"

"Three SWAT teams from Orlando are on ready alert. Their assembly point will be the St. Lucie Airport a few miles north of Fort Pierce. Hostage Rescue units from Miami are also on call if needed."

"Make a note," Nurkiewicz said. "Glenner wants us to request Cobra helicopters from Patrick Air Force Base."

"No sweat. I'll take care of it," Manion replied. "In the meantime we sit with our thumbs up our asses, waiting."

Nurkiewicz wagged a chunky finger. "When we nail that Israeli fucker, it will be a career sweetener for me, kudos for this department, and no more bullshit about cutting our budget."

A puzzled frown crossed Manion's face.

...43

AT THREE A.M., FERNANDEZ turned over in bed. He fumbled open his iPhone one-handed.

"It's me, Latisha."

"Oh," he grumbled. "Hi."

"You promised to call."

"I had a lot on my mind," he mumbled sleepily. "I spent the day in Florida with an assassin, my job is in the toilet, and my flight arrived two hours late."

"Oh, puh-lease."

"Hang on a minute." He went into the bathroom to urinate. Fernandez looked at his reflection in the mirror over the sink. He could make out the deep circles etched beneath his eyes, even in the pale bathroom light.

"I'm back."

"Frank. My father remembered the name Cesar Zúñiga."

"Great," he fumed, feeling the anger roil. "For that hot flash, you woke me up in the middle of the night. Goodbye."

"Wait, Frank. Don't you dare hang up on me. The reason my father remembered Cesar Zúñiga's name was because he said that the FBI was no better than the CIA."

"I don't understand."

"I contacted my father's administrative assistant, Karen Wexler. Karen knows all the secret switches to find information in Washington. She e-mailed me the information. Splash some water on your face and let me read it to you.

"Panama's General Manuel Antonio Noriega worked with the U.S. Central Intelligence Agency from the late 1950s until the 1980s. In 1988 grand juries in Florida indicted him on U.S. federal drug charges. In 1988, a subcommittee

120

concluded that the CIA had a relationship with the Panamanian drug lord Noriega and turned a blind eye to his corruption and drug dealing, even as he emerged as a key player on behalf of the Medellín Cartel."

"What does Noriega have to do with Zúñiga?"

"Karen told me she found out that in closed-door testimony before Dad's subcommittee, it was revealed that a high-level player closely associated with a narco-trafficking organization in Colombia had been working with the FBI. Guess the identity of the player? It was Cesar Zúñiga."

"*Jesus Christ!*"

"According to Karen, the FBI supported Cesar Zúñiga as part of an anti-drug strategy to weaken the major drug kingpins in Colombia. The Bureau claimed credit for abetting the killing of the Medillin's Pablo Escobar and the retirement of the Ocha brothers of the Cali. When the gangsters in Colombia split into mini-cartels, Zúñiga's Cartagena cartel took control. The FBI's complicity is spelled out in the committee's classified report."

Fernandez' heart pounded. "Who was Zúñiga's handler?"

…44

"YOUR GUN AND BADGE." Nurkiewicz' face turned a deep shade of red. He reminded Fernandez of a mini J. Edgar Hoover. "Did you, for just one goddamn minute, think that it was within your authority *not* to tell your superior officer that you knew the identity and current location of one of the world's most wanted criminals?"

"I met Uri Rechmann. He's an old man—"

"*You met him!*" Nurkiewicz echoed. "*You met him*! By now he is probably in Mexico."

"No. The target is still in place, boss," Manion said. "He picked up the morning paper and watered his flowers; doesn't seem in a rush to go anywhere. The target's wife drove off twenty minutes ago. I have a unit following her. She's shopping in a Publix supermarket."

"You don't understand," Fernandez explained. "Rechmann had no connection to the Mafia. He—"

Nurkiewicz cut him off. "Effective immediately, Fernandez, you are on indefinite suspension—without pay or health benefits. And as soon as this operation is concluded, I want your desk cleared out or you will face charges. Got that?"

Fernandez inhaled deeply. He did not reply.

"People like you aren't cut out for the FBI. You're not a team player, Fernandez. You're a bleeding-heart whistle-blower. You people—"

"You mean Hispanics?"

Nurkiewicz's intercom buzzed softly.

"Mr. N," Latisha said softly. "There's a telephone intercept from Fort Pierce, Florida. I think you guys need to listen to it."

"Señor Zúñiga?"

122

"Yes."

"This is Marcus Wolffe calling."

"Thank you for telephoning, Mr. Wolffe. I am honored that you have contacted me at this time, because I am planning to return to Colombia in a few days."

"Senor Zúñiga, you mentioned in our last conversation that in view of the Tampa situation, you are considering new representation in the state of Florida. It would be a pleasure to have you visit my home. We would have privacy. One can't be too careful these days. My wife will be at work tomorrow evening."

"What time would be most convenient?"

"Eight o'clock."

"Until then, sir. Goodbye."

"Do you know what this means?" Manion slapped his hand on the armrest. "Now we can move on Rechmann without Interpol's or Justice's permission. Zúñiga is a wanted drug dealer. That's our legal justification for the raid." He winked. "If we happen to net a wanted international criminal in the operation, well, surprise, surprise."

Nurkiewicz hesitated, a squint of confusion in his eyes.

A knot formed in Fernandez' stomach. He studied Nurkiewicz's reaction closely.

"Thank you, Latisha," Nurkiewicz said, excusing himself. He closed the conference room door and went into his own office.

"What's that all about?" Manion asked.

Fernandez shrugged. "You saw the photo of Rechmann with the fisherman on the beach. The guy in the picture was Alex Lindsay, head of CIA's Black Ops. Before you launch the raid, you better touch base with the CIA."

"What does the damn CIA have to do with anything?" Nurkiewicz barked upon reentering the room.

"Uri Rechmann told me he had worked with the CIA."

"Right. And if your mother had balls, she would be your father." The venom in the man's voice startled Fernandez.

"Glenner gave the OK," Nurkiewicz said. "Ready to roll?"

"No problem," Manion replied, his voice cool. "Target's still in place. The Zúñiga meeting is set for eight o'clock. That's good. Nighttime may help keep civilians off the streets. All units are assembling at St. Lucie Airport at 0500. Agents dressed as UPS drivers will escort neighbors a safe distance away.

"Two SWAT teams of 42 members each will be utilized. Team Alpha will assemble on the property in a nearby condominium. The Beta team will make use of a clubhouse called Aruba. Both buildings have side or rear entrances that cannot be seen from the target's line of sight."

"Contingency plans?"

"You know Murphy's Law," Manion continued. "If something can go wrong, it probably will. If we end up with a hostage situation, our FBI Hostage Rescue Team is stationed two miles away. If it's a barricade situation, we will wait it out, unless they open fire on us or on civilians; then, on your orders, the SWAT units will launch an assault to end the standoff."

Nurkiewicz pumped his fist. "OK. Let's move out."

Why would Rechmann remain in his home? Fernandez wondered. *He knows about the FBI tap. Does the old man have a death wish?*

...45

HE INHALED THE FAINT AROMA of Latisha's perfume as he unlocked his front door.

"I don't usually date out-of-work guys."

He smiled a tired smile and sat down next to her on the sofa. He patted her thigh and left his hand there.

"Do you ever think of doing something else?"

"Every day. But I don't know what that would be."

"Are you OK?"

"Not really. If Zúñiga had an FBI handler, I'm concerned that information about the Fort Pierce raid will be leaked—again. And I find it passing strange that Nurkiewicz adamantly refused to communicate with the CIA."

"Why would he do that?"

Fernandez shook his head. "Only two people knew details of the Miami operation: Richard Nurkiewicz and Charlie Manion. For Nurkiewicz, nailing Zúñiga would have been a feather in his cap, and that man collects cap feathers like Custer collected scalps. He had everything to gain for the operation to be successful.

"Charlie Manion managed our Miami office. He held a personal grudge against me, but Charlie is an FBI pro. I can't believe he would tip off Zúñiga." He paused. "Today Nurkiewicz left the room for a few minutes. I'm getting paranoid."

"Daddy has this neat trick of explaining things with one single question, which is *who benefits*?"

"So?"

"If Mr. N. is involved with Zúñiga, *how* does he benefit? What if I asked Karen to use her *special* sources and quietly check into our boss's bank accounts?"

Fernandez wasn't listening. "I'm out of a job and it's my own fault, but I'm proud to have worked for the FBI. Anyone would

be." He looked at Latisha and smiled. "The Bureau is an organization in need of competent young people—like yourself, particularly
women and lawyers. Maybe you have an interest?"

"No. But I'm curious how hard it is for women to get in."

"It's not a cakewalk. We had a special problem with one lady.
A few years ago at Quantico I ran three candidates through their final
test. I took the first male applicant to a large metal door and handed
him a gun. I told him, "The Bureau must know that you will follow
instructions no matter what the circumstances. Inside the room you
will find your wife sitting in a chair. Kill her!"

Latisha's eyes widened.

"The applicant said, 'You can't be serious! I could never
shoot my wife!' I told him right out, "Then you're not the right man
for this job. Take your wife and go home.

"I gave the second guy the same instructions. He took the
gun and went into the room. All was quiet for about five minutes.
Then he came out with tears in his eyes. He told me he really tried,
but couldn't kill his wife. I explained that in the FBI, sacrifices
have to be made to keep our country free.

"Finally, the female applicant came in. I gave her the same
instructions. She took the gun and went into the room. Shots were
heard, one after another. We heard screaming, crashing, banging on
the walls. After a few minutes, everything quieted down. The door
opened slowly and there stood the woman. She wiped the sweat
from her brow. 'This gun is loaded with blanks,' she told me. 'I
had to beat him to death with the chair.' "

Latisha punched his shoulder. "You had me for a minute."

"I would like to have you—for more than a minute."

Her breath fell in small bursts as she nodded, unbuttoned
her blouse and wiggled free from it like a teenager. She grasped his
head in both hands and kissed him on the mouth, first without the
tongue, and then with it. Fernandez stroked her throat lightly, moving down over the swell of her breasts. He felt light-headed as he

enveloped her with both arms. They kissed for a long time. He removed his tie and shirt. Latisha lifted up so he could take off her bra. He had some trouble with the clasp, then mumbled, "Here we go." She let him look and touch her. He kissed her shoulder blade and one of her dark nipples. "That's nice," she purred.

He got out of his clothes, and when he turned back to her he saw Latisha naked too. They embraced atop the sofa. She brought her hand up to caress the twin pinkish scars on his chest. They kissed again, slowly, tenderly at first, then deeply with abandon, her tongue sliding against his teeth, probing deeper. He could smell perfume on her skin and her hair.

They had crossed the line of agent-intern that he had firmly drawn. He no longer worked for the FBI. He kissed her mouth and rubbed himself between her thighs. She moaned beneath him and laughed softly and with pleasure as his fingers found her swollen spot. Her skin was a very deep brown against his tan body. And then she dropped off the sofa, down on the floor, murmuring something in a soft, kittenish voice, but he couldn't understand it because she was also taking his penis into her mouth.

One hour later, Fernandez rolled off of his sofa with a happy smile. He carried the sleeping Latisha into the bedroom. He was fit and kept in shape with regular visits to the gym, but the previous hour had required most of his stamina. He put on underwear and took the dossier into the living room, yawning. He brewed coffee and began to review the file on Uri Rechmann, assassin, ex-Shivaman, ex-Marcus Wolffe.

In 1984, Rechmann became the prime suspect in the sudden death of a popular radical cleric known for inflammatory pro-al-Qaeda speeches, Mullah Abu-Nazari. The Mullah's corpse was found in his own backyard with a bullet hole in the center of his forehead. It became international news for one day, quickly overcome by the continuing civil war in the western Darfur region.

In 2001, Hani M. al-Juhani, one of the organizers of the 2000 attack on the *USS Cole*, was shot in the head and killed in Yemen. Arab newspapers claimed CIA involvement in the assassination. Washington rejected the claim.

After 2002, the assassin known as Uri Rechmann, or "Shivaman," became a legend in the Middle East. Attacks included the assassination of bomb-maker Massoud Aziz Al-Dakheel outside his Tehran workshop in 2003, and Fereydoun Shahriari, head of Iran's Atomic Energy organization, in January 2006.

In 2005, in Kabul, Afghanistan, the Allied forces commander, British General Gerald Hankins, reported that the legendary assassin Uri Rechmann had died in a mysterious explosion. Body never recovered.

...46

"WE HAVE SET UP TWO CAMERA LOCATIONS," the technician in the FBI's control room explained. The young man in a blue blazer had shaken their hands politely, but warily. "My name's Davies, Dennis Davies."

The technician obviously had been briefed on Fernandez' tenuous status and the presence of Congressman Du Burn's daughter. He introduced them to a balding, stoop-shouldered man with a three-piece dark blue suit and a precise manner, accentuated by a toothbrush mustache and rimless glasses. The gentleman identified himself as Winston Peartree, the Bureau's public relations officer. Peartree shook hands without rising. Frank dumped himself down into a chair. Latisha sat down opposite him, brushing a breast against his shoulder for an instant. Clusters of glasses and coffee cups cluttered the small conference room table.

The tech pressed a switch on his console. Across the room a teak panel glided silently sideways to reveal a full HD, 50-inch, plasma color TV screen. Uri Rechmann's house swam into focus. "Camera One is implanted with our Alpha team in a condominium unit," Davies exclaimed, pausing to refer to his notes.

"Place is called Ocean Villas II. Notice that from this vantage point we have an unobstructed view of the front of the target's house. Our second location is set up in a clubhouse called the Aruba Center." He clicked the remote. "View from Camera Two covers the back area of the house and the lawn leading down thirty yards to water on the golf course."

"What is your job?" Frank asked Peartree.

"If we don't feed the media beast, it will feed on *us*," Peartree puffed. "After the Waco disaster, we learned that the FBI must have a consistent message with one voice, either the director's or his designated spokesperson, namely me. If we cannot provide information in a timely manner during a crisis, the media will look elsewhere because of deadlines and the urgency associated with filling the public's need for 24-hour news."

Fernandez tasted the surprisingly pleasant coffee. His smile faded. "That's not the only thing we learned from Waco. You also have to be certain that the information you provide is *true*."

Peartree scowled. "Hold on a minute—"

The technician broke in, "Heads up. We have bogies."

On the screen, Frank saw a black Cadillac moving slowly along Windward Drive, pausing at the corner for a few minutes before crawling into Uri Rechmann's driveway.

"Can you pan it in closer?"

Davies nodded, making adjustments.

Cesar Zúñiga got out of the vehicle. Two muscled body-guards escorted the drug lord to Rechmann's front entrance. One was a very large, barrel-chested man with a close-cropped black beard and olive complexion. The other man was short but beefy. Frank noticed the short hoodlum adjusting a gun under his left arm. At close range, he could make out the rough texture of Zúñiga's pockmarked face. The front door opened. Frank watched as Rechmann greeted his guests.

"It's showtime," Davies pronounced, studying his watch.

THE RAID ON RECHMANN'S HOUSE began exactly at 8:15 P.M. Everyone in the control room gaped at the screen. After a split second of hesitation, people with helmets on their heads and shotguns in their hands were seen moving with the practiced efficiency of an elite SWAT team readying itself for action. Fernandez watched them, impressed with what he saw. The two SWAT teams moved silently into position—lights out, black-on-black. The strict ban on speech and flashlights meant he could hear no sounds nor see any lights.

Precisely at 8:15, floodlights lit up the front and back of Rechmann's house like daylight. Fernandez heard a familiar voice.

"This is the FBI!" Nurkiewicz's voice boomed over a bull-horn. "The house is completely surrounded. Come out with your hands up. You have exactly one minute."

The tension felt palpable in the room. Latisha dug her nails into Fernandez's arm. Davies amplified the sound reception. For the briefest moment, everything was unnaturally quiet. No traffic noises could be heard thrumming from A1A; cars and trucks had been diverted. Fernandez saw jagged lightning flashes. He heard thunderclaps in the distance, somewhere over Lake Okeechobee.

On the TV screen, Nurkiewicz could be seen striding away from the protection of the police car in a military fashion. He raised his bullhorn again. "You inside. Zúñiga. This is your last chance be-fore—"

Suddenly, they heard an explosion. Automatic weapon fire came from the direction of the house. A volley sprayed in Nurkie-wicz's direction. The camera shifted to the shooter standing behind an open window, shadowy and indistinct. Fernandez saw Nurkie-wicz trying to flatten himself behind the police car.

"Be careful, you fool," Fernandez yelled.

"It's an Uzi submachine gun," the tech said, surprised.

Someone from the direction of the house loosed a brief burst. Nurkiewicz took the blast in his chest. He sagged against the vehicle, his front a wash of blood. Voices could be heard shouting, "Leader down."

THE STANDOFF LASTED OVER ONE HOUR. The people in the control room learned that Richard Nurkiewicz had been taken by ambulance to Lawnwood Regional Hospital. His condition remained guarded.

Fernandez noticed furtive movement by FBI SWAT team members. He heard the familiar muffled pops of canisters being fired into the front and back windows. "Oh, my God!" Fernandez breathed. "Not M651 tear gas."

Frozen in his seat, he heard a telltale *whomp-whomp-whomp.* Davies went to a split-screen. From the Aruba camera, two AH-1 Cobra helicopters rose out of the moonlit sky. The Cobras banked through the stiff offshore winds, shuddering in the crosscurrents. Fernandez watched in horror. Flames leaped from the airship's wings as they fired pinpointed Hellfire missiles.

An ear-splitting explosion jolted Uri Rechmann's house, like a bomb going off. The explosion lit the Florida night sky with a blazing orange light. A cloud of smoke spewed upward. Then a billowing ball of flame tore up into the sky.

Fernandez was paralyzed by shock and disbelief, staring at the scene of total destruction being transmitted. He heard the distinctive wail of fire engines. On the screen came a close-up shot of a man wearing a black helmet, a black jumpsuit and an armored vest. Fernandez recognized Charlie Manion. Manion held some kind of assault weapon and wore a radio headset, a thin bar curving in front of his mouth.

"Actions taken as ordered, sir," Manion reported. "Casualty Report: Deputy Director Nurkiewicz is down, and we have two walking wounded. The local fire department is on their way. Over and out."

Fernandez shook with rage. He felt tears coming.

…47

THE RED CALL BUTTON LIT UP.

ROSALIE: "Domestic Violence hotline. How can we help?"

CALLER: "Remember me, Miss Rose? My name is Joyce."

ROSALIE: "Of course I do, Joyce. Are you OK?"

CALLER: "Since Eugene *fell off the ladder*, he's stopped slapping me around. I wanted to call and say, God bless."

ROSALIE: "Domestic Violence hotline."

CALLER: "My name is Sarah."

ROSALIE: "OK, Sarah, what's the problem?"

CALLER: "The man I live with is a drunk. When he drinks, he beats up on me."

ROSALIE: "If you are not married, why don't you leave the man?"

CALLER: "There ain't no jobs out there, lady. How am I going to feed my family?"

ROSALIE: "I know times are tough. Give me your address, Sarah."

Rosalie spoke to the new police recruit, a good-looking officer with dreamy blue eyes. "Do me a favor, sweetheart," she said, handing him the caller's name and address. "This woman is being threatened by her husband. Please check it out."

"Yes, ma'am. I'll get right on it."

As Rosalie returned to her post, she heard Ronnie punching numbers into his mobile phone and issuing instructions. "Dispatch to Echo-Twenty."

Ten minutes later, the door opened and Jessica Towers, the state attorney, entered, followed by a somber-faced Ronnie and two other Fort Pierce police officers.

"Mrs. Wolffe," Towers said somberly, "I'm afraid that I have dreadful news."

...48

FBI Man Wounded In Drug Raid

THE WASHINGTON POST—FBI Deputy Director Richard Nurkiewicz was seriously wounded during a roundup of major drug trafficking suspects in Fort Pierce, Florida. FBI SWAT teams converged on a residence in an oceanside community on Hutchinson Island at 8:15 Tuesday. Deputy Director Richard Nurkiewicz continues to recover from multiple bullet wounds. He is listed in stable condition and is expected to make a full recovery.

On the evening of the raid, startled Ocean Village residents watched anxiously as U.S. Army Cobra helicopters fired Hellfire missiles into the single dwelling house in their quiet neighborhood. Neighbor Estelle Dobbin was quoted as saying, "I looked out of my window and saw a SWAT team on my lawn. It was just like in the movies." Resident Herman Pustin added, "I think I heard an FBI guy got shot, not sure."

FBI Public Relations Officer Winston Peartree ignored questions from the media, claiming that the FBI's inspection team would launch an investigation, which could take a couple of weeks. The process is already underway. Peartree added, "In the FBI, our whole purpose is to serve the public, and we love the job we do every day."

Fort Pierce Police sources report they were not apprised of the raid in advance. Occupants of the house at the time of the raid were believed to be

Cesar Zúñiga, a major narco-trafficker, two of his bodyguards, and the owner of the property, Mr. Marcus Wolffe, suspected of having close ties to the Mafia.

.

...49

BLOOD DRAINED FROM HIS FACE as Fernandez read the *Post* article. Not a single mention of Uri Rechmann. When the phone rang, he let the answering machine take the call.

"I know you're there, Frank. We need to talk. Pick up the phone. It's important."

"Talk away."

"Karen Wexler checked into Nurkiewicz' bank accounts."

"And?"

"Nothing out of the ordinary. Uh... she also checked into your accounts."

Puzzled, he asked, "Why mine, for Christ's sake?"

"Karen called it 'doing due diligence.' She found out that you were barely scraping by, but she also checked other senior FBI officials." Latisha paused. "Frank, I don't know how to tell you this. Karen uncovered one with sizable offshore holdings in the Bahamas, very, very sizable. Maybe it is a remarkable coincidence, but you taught me not to believe in coincidences. Right?"

A light sweat beaded his forehead. In his secret heart, he knew. Fernandez leaned forward and buried his face in his hands. He breathed deeply several times; then he raised his face. "It's—"

"Yes. Your best friend, Director William Glenner."

JUST BEFORE 4:00 P.M., Fernandez brushed by the FBI director's protesting praetorian guard.

"Don't bother knocking, Frank," Glenner sighed with an edge to his voice, clearly annoyed. *"Cómo está usted?"*

"Bill. You were the one who leaked to Zúñiga?"

"Don't take it personally, pal. Leaking is a varsity sport in Washington. The gods of political expediency needed to be satisfied. Protecting Zúñiga was a risk–benefit analysis. It took years, but we finally cleaned out Cali and Escobar." He shrugged. "I never thought it would end the way it did, with you getting nearly killed. Hindsight is 20/20. In my job sometimes I need to do what I need to do, so the Bureau can get the funding and political backing for what guys like you need to do."

"I don't think so." He felt the air had gone out of the room.

Glenner continued, "We are at war with terrorists and drug cartels. That's what we learned from 9/11: al Qaeda is not the Cosa Nostra, and Osama bin Laden wasn't a John Gotti—"

Fernandez interrupted. "Don't wave the flag to me. You also leaked that I uncovered the truth about Waco. I was the disloyal whistle-blower, while you went to the attorney general as Mr. Clean."

"It's history, Frank. Don't let it eat you up."

Fernandez inhaled slowly. "Tell me, *Semper Fi* buddy, did you also order Manion to fire the canisters and call in the Cobras?"

The director rose to his feet, plainly angry, his voice rising. "When hostile fire was visited upon officers in the performance of their assigned duties and serious injuries were sustained, it became my responsibility to protect lives. That's exactly what I did."

"And you eliminated Zúñiga, so that no one could ever testify against you."

Glenner faced Fernandez with an expression of purest contempt. His hands started to tremble; rage cracked his habitual self-control. "I don't owe you any explanations. I protected your Hispanic ass for years, and this is the gratitude I get?" Glenner made an irritable gesture of dismissal.

Fernandez allowed himself a small smile. "By the way. I found it unusual that Rechmann's death was not mentioned in the media. The CIA asked you to deep-six it."

"In this business, one hand washes the other."

"You mean laundering, don't you?"

"Ah, the money," he said, giving Fernandez a feral smile.

"You are finished, Bill. Congressman Du Burns knows about the drug payoffs stashed in your offshore accounts."

"That problem has been contained."

Fernandez' heart sank. "Du Burns is not taking action?"

"In Washington, everybody has to make a living. A favor offered is a favor returned."

"So now what?" Fernandez asked. "Do you resign?"

"What happens," Glenner told him flatly, "is that you get the fuck out of my office, out of my Bureau and out of my life. Now! Before I call security."

...50

THE NEXT DAY FERNANDEZ EMPTIED HIS DESK, clearing out bits and pieces, shredding outdated documents and correspondence. The mementos that made the final cut were swept into two large paper shopping bags. He took a last look around, inhaled a deep breath and turned off the lights.

With bags in hand, he walked down the labyrinthine corridor past Nurkiewicz's open door. Fernandez saw Charlie Manion sitting behind the desk. He stepped in.

"A promotion?"

"Temporary assignment," Manion said without looking up.

"How's Nurk doing?"

"The asshole wouldn't listen. He didn't wear a vest. Scuttlebutt has it that he'll receive the Medal for Meritorious Achievement—the same one his father got."

"I watched on closed circuit. You did a good job, Charlie."

Manion shrugged. He noted the two shopping bags. "I don't mind telling you, Fernandez, that I'm glad you're leaving. Every time I see your face it reminds me—"

Fernandez held up both hands. "I understand."

"No. Unless you experience something yourself, you can never understand."

"The same goes for bullet fragments lodged in your chest."

"Touché. Now excuse me, I have a ton of paperwork."

Fernandez had just picked up his shopping bags when the phone rang. Manion listened carefully, jotting down notes. "Are you absolutely certain?" he asked, his brows knit.

"What?" Fernandez asked.

"After the raid, thunderstorms blew in from the west. The forensic team was able to collect the charred remains sooner than expected. They bagged every last crumb of debris for analysis, part

140

of it human. The ME called to report they have positively DNA identified the three Colombians' bodies. Zúñiga's was the most interesting because he had a large skull."

"I don't understand."

"What I am trying to get into your thick Hispanic brain is that someone put a bullet hole in the center of Zúñiga's—between the brows."

Fernandez opened his mouth wide. "And the fourth body?"

"Apparently, at the moment of explosion, Rechmann must have been in the least sheltered place of the house—the kitchen. Under the rubble the forensic team could only find numerous slivers of human bone."

"What do you make of all this?"

"It's above my pay grade," Manion snorted. "But something is fishy. Why wasn't Rechmann's name mentioned in the FBI's press release?"

"I won't try and defend Uri Rechmann. He had blood on his hands handling black contracts for many governments—including ours. He told me that he had records stored in safe hands that upon his death would reveal complicity in high quarters. For that reason, important people internationally don't want him around, and they don't want his death reported. They want him in indefinite limbo."

Manion narrowed his eyes. "The Bureau rumor mill is grinding in high gear. Want to share anything before you go not so gently into the civilian world?"

"I go without rage, Charlie, just sadness."

"Word is that Glenner is dirty and that he's retiring to live in the Virgin Islands."

"I hadn't heard that."

"And the word also is that you made it happen." Manion stood up to shake hands. "Personally, I think you are a shit, Fernandez, but professionally you have been a credit to the FBI."

But with his empty outstretched hand, Manion was talking to the closed door.

FERNANDEZ TOTED HIS BAGS toward the elevator. Colleagues gave him mock salutes and secretaries nodded with thin smiles. He rode to the ground floor and let himself out through the turnstiles with his laminated ID. No guard paused to check the bags as he left the building for the last time.

Now what? Fernandez mused, feeling a shortness of breath and regretting that he had never developed any absorbing hobbies, like Uri Rechmann, who bred daylilies. He loosened his tie and crumpled his jacket into one of the large paper bags. Could he make his way without the Bureau and the peer group of agents among whom he had worked for most of his adult life? He loved Washington; it had more monuments, woods, trees, parks and gardens than any city he knew.

Despite his best efforts, he thought about Latisha, unable to get her off of his mind. He also felt starved, not having had lunch. He punched in her number.

"You hungry?"

"Sure, I guess. How did it go?"

"I am now gainfully unemployed."

"Can you afford to buy me dinner?"

"Chiang's?"

"Give me an hour. I'm tied up at the moment."

"SAKE, PLEASE, HOT," Latisha told the waitress.

Fernandez ordered the same.

She eyed him curiously. "Tell me everything."

THE ORANGE BLOSSOM MOB

"Manion received the preliminary forensic report. Three corpses have been positively identified as Zúñiga's and his two bodyguards'." He paused to down his sake.

"Did they find Rechmann's body?"

He shrugged. "The forensic people found shards of human bone in the area that took the brunt of the missile hits."

"What aren't you telling me?"

"Zúñiga's skull had a bullet hole in the forehead."

"My God! Rechmann killed Zúñiga?"

He nodded, but didn't respond.

"Is it possible that Rechmann could still be alive?"

"No way. You saw that the inferno. SWAT teams covered all sides of the house. There were no secret tunnels, and they found slivers of bone in the kitchen area."

"I'm a law school graduate," she countered. "Lawyers like specificity. Did the forensic team make a DNA identification of Rechmann's body? Yes or no?"

"If they did, Manion didn't say. What's your point?"

"Do you remember telling me about the hitman named George Fangman?"

"What about him?"

"They recovered his head—but not his body."

Fernandez laughed. "Let's order."

"WHAT ARE YOUR PLANS?" Latisha asked.

"I saw an ad, a small security agency for sale in Fort Pierce, the Orange Blossom something or other. I'm thinking about making an offer. I like warm weather; I'm fluent in Spanish. I'm an experienced investigator. Why not give it a try?" He took a deep breath. "Latisha, I know we have an age difference, but—"

"Hold on, honey," she broke in. "Don't go there. I like the sex, but I'm too young to bury myself in some redneck town in Florida. My internship is up, and I might get involved in politics."

Fernandez could feel something gnawing away in his stomach. "Why didn't your father expose Glenner? Congressman Du Burns had the offshore banking evidence."

"Daddy doesn't tell me everything." She paused. He saw her decide to lie. He could sense it: a barely noticeable shift in Latisha's voice, a sudden insecurity in her eyes—enough for Fernandez to register it.

"Tell me the truth."

She shrugged. "I'm going to work for my father."

He persisted. "Let me ask you again: why didn't your father turn Glenner over to the attorney general?"

Latisha eyed him shrewdly. "We were sitting in this very restaurant when you told me that if someone violated a confidence, they were nothing but a snitch."

His heart sank. He realized what Glenner had meant: his problem *had been* contained. He tossed a twenty-dollar bill on the table. "Goodbye, Latisha."

51

Secrecy Shrouds Du Burns' "Super Pac"

THE NEW YORK TIMES—Newly disclosed details confirm rumors of millions of dollars flowing into the recently established super-PAC of announced presidential primary hopeful, Congressman Clarence Du Burns of Louisiana.

Some of the money came from companies closely identified with Du Burns, like the giant British oil company BP LLC, whose deepwater well gushed thousands of gallons of oil daily into the Gulf of Mexico. Another major donor named is the Houston based Halliburton Co.

Such donations were made possible by the Supreme Court's Citizen's United decision in 2010 and subsequent court rulings, which opened the door to unlimited corporate and union contributions to political committees and made it possible to pool that money with unlimited contributions from wealthy individuals. Group supporters of each party employ techniques that allow them to cloak the identities of many of their donors.

The pro-Du Burns super PAC is reported to have received a two million dollar check from a major supporter. The nonprofit organization listed their address in campaign finance records as a post office box in Charlotte Amalie East in the U. S. Virgin Islands.

"While we know some names of people giving megabucks, we know nothing about the funders of the nonprofits," concluded Heidi Sachs, the executive director of the Sunlight Foundation, which advocates greater transparency in political giving. She added, "We don't know what we don't know, and the Du Burns super-PAC is a prime example."

52

"WITH BERNIE GONE, things ain't the same," Bats Battaglia said as he turned off Virginia Avenue and slowly cruised down Oleander. "I might as well get my knees fixed. There's a doc in Vero does both at the same time."

Crazy Sal Scarlotti echoed the idea. "I can't handle being out 'til 3 A.M., then getting up and driving forty miles to Lake Okeechobee by sunup and fishing all day. I'm gettin' too old for this shit. Fishing is big right now from Pelican Bay all the way up to Cochran's Pass; water temperature in the upper seventies, and with the full moon next week, the fucking bass will be jumping in the boat."

Battaglia yelled, "Catch a look at that guy in the dark clothes. He's the one Vesta told us about who just got out of jail!"

"Come here, buddy," Sal said. "What's your name, kid?"

The young man seemed genuinely surprised to be stopped. "My name is Richard Sandford, sir."

Scarlotti glanced at him sharply. "Why are you walking around at 2 A.M., Richard?"

"Insomnia. I couldn't sleep."

"Where do you live?"

Sanford seemed puzzled with the question. "Bell Avenue."

"Ain't that a pretty far distance from here, kid?"

The young man shrugged. He didn't answer.

"What are you carrying on you?" Sal asked.

"Just my flashlight and screwdriver," Sanford smiled. "But that don't prove nothing."

Battaglia gripped his cane. "Get in, kid," he said. "We'll drop you off."

"Why?" Sanford asked suspiciously.

"It's a long hike to the emergency room, kid."

TWO NIGHTS LATER, BIG MIKE De Luca sipped his black coffee in the Hess gas station parking lot on Okeechobee Road. "I can't be out all night like this," he complained. "Then get up and make tee time at 8 A.M.—"

"Hold it, Mike," Rizzo broke in. "Call's coming in." Rizzo fiddled with the Midland two-way VHF police radio he had liberated from the police parking lot.

Dispatch to all cars. A robbery has been reported at the WalMart Supercenter 5100 on Okeechobee Road. Two male suspects discharged weapons and fled on foot headed east. No casualties reported. One man is believed to be a white male wearing a hooded top and cargo pants. The second suspect reported wearing a multi-colored hat and a black coat. An unknown amount of money reported stolen. Suspects are to be considered armed and dangerous.

"WalMart's a mile or so west of here. Wanna take a look-see?" Eddie Rizzo asked. De Luca nodded and drove the van into Pineapple Plaza. Rizzo put in helpfully, "Those mugs wouldn't be stupid enough to run down the main drag." Blue police lights flashed by as they turned into the strip mall. He had ventured only a little way in when two figures came out of the darkness.

"Out of the car," the black man yelled. His hair under the multicolored cap looked black and glossy. His skin was dark and his cheekbones were high and flat.

"Give us your car—nobody gets hurt," the white man in the hood said.

Rizzo pressed a button and the passenger window descended. "We are lost, young fellow. Can you help us?"

The large white man, still breathing heavily, leaned into the window. "We haven't time to fuck around, Grandpa—"

Eddie Rizzo leaned forward, drew the loop of wire from his pocket and whipped it around the man's neck. The garrote proved to be fast, silent and effective. The white male dropped on the hardtop street, a bulging WalMart plastic bag by his side.

In a swift, unexpected surge, De Luca shoved open the car door into the other man's stomach. The robber was tough. He grunted, but retained his grip on his gun. De Luca jumped out of the car fast and hit him on the jaw. And he hit him hard. Then he thrust his elbows into the black man's ribs, cupped a hand over his mouth and punched him twice, hard, on the back of his head. With the first hit, the guy gurgled; with the second he passed out. And for the briefest moment, everything was quiet.

"Waddaya think?" he asked Eddie Rizzo. "The Gators?"

Rizzo nodded and smiled. "Guess what, Joe? We're rich."

Walmart Robbers Escape With Cash

TREASURE COAST PRESS—Fort Pierce Police are investigating a robbery at the WalMart Supercenter, 5100 Okeechobee Road. Police reported that shortly before the store closed at 11:55 P.M. on Wednesday, two men entered the supercenter carrying handguns and demanded money. The suspects fired two shots. No one was injured, and the suspects fled on foot with an unknown amount of money.

One of the suspects is described as a white male wearing a black mask, black gloves, dark colored hoodie, light colored pants with cargo type pockets and white Nike tennis shoes. The other suspect is a black male wearing an orange, brown and green knit cap, sunglasses, black coat, black jeans, black gloves and black shoes.

Police believe that a third individual may have been involved driving a getaway vehicle. Anyone with information about the robbery or the suspects is asked to call Fort Pierce Police at 772-461-3820.

...54

EDWARD AND DOLLY RIZZO entered the colorful teal green stuccoed A. E. Backus Museum on Indian River Drive.

"Now that we can afford it," Dolly whispered, "we should join the museum and mix with a better class of people than those geriatric mobsters you pal around with." Eddie Rizzo let her rave on, knowing that he couldn't tell her the money had come from WalMart and not the Florida Lottery.

"Mr. Rizzo. We welcome new members," explained Robin De Mornay, the A. E. Backus Museum's marketing director. "This is the most important exhibition we've ever put together. A once-in-a-lifetime opportunity to see the full range of A.E. Backus' craft as it evolved through the decades."

Rizzo puzzled over whether it was polite to dip his shrimp twice in the cocktail sauce.

"This show includes more than fifty A. E. Backus paintings," the museum director continued. "Many works are from private collections and are rarely available for public viewing."

"What does his stuff go for?" Eddie asked.

"Depends. Many of Backus' earlier paintings dating from the 1930s to the late 1960s are categorized as being more impressionistic than most of his later works. Backus was the first artist to truly see the subtle beauty of Florida and to attempt to capture it on canvas. He is considered to be the seminal Florida landscape painter—"

"How much?" Rizzo broke in.

"Between $35,000 and $100,000."

"I don't see no guards."

Robin De Mornay lowered her voice. "We probably should have more security. You see the picture of Marilyn Monroe at the end of the hall? Well, that is an original Andy Warhol on loan from the Detroit Museum. That one is worth five million."

Ex-con Eddie Rizzo felt his stomach churning. "Five million dollars," he echoed softly. "You have an alarm system?"

"We have alarm sensors on all doors and windows in the gallery. One part of the sensor has a magnet; the other is a circuit with a metal switch that keeps the magnet closed. This system prevents intruders from being able to cut the wires attached to the sensors and disable the alarm. If someone didn't know the code and tried to break in, the circuit would break and trigger the alarm."

"And as marketing director, you have the code?" he inquired politely.

Robin De Mornay smiled and patted her purse.

Fast Eddie Rizzo raised his eyes. *Thank you, Jesus.*

THE GOLF THREESOME crossed Gator Trace Drive, pulling their golf carts to the tenth tee. Big Mike De Luca was up first—he had the honors. De Luca took out his new Callaway titanium driver with the hyperbolic face technology created for long distance and specially designed to prevent slicing.

Standing on the tee box, Big Mike paused. *Don't think about the water; eyes on the ball; keep your ass down.* He took a breath, dragged his left arm back slowly, then pivoted and powered through the swing. The ball sailed high and long and straight, landing 300 yards down the center of the fairway.

"Nice hit, Mike," Joey Culotta called out.

"*Jesus.*" Sam Barbosa held his nose. "What's that odor?"

The golfers were interrupted when a truck pulled up along the edge of the water. Two men hopped out. Large lettering on the side of their vehicle spelled out St. Lucie County Animal Control Services. The driver looked short and stumpy, like a fire hydrant.

"Sorry to interrupt your game, guys," he shouted. The animal removal team pushed a four-foot metal platform truck to the water's edge. They fastened ropes around the carcass of a dead alligator and then struggled to push the dolly back to their van.

"It's good for our business," the driver said, his face covered with sweat. "But I sure as shit hate to see these fat old gators become an endangered species." He gave a mock salute and backed the truck away.

"It's the fuckin' global warming killing the gators," Joey Culotta insisted. "That's what it is."

"No. I heard it was the *El Niño,*" Sam Barbosa said.

"They'll probably put in swans or something and change the name to Swan Lake Golf course," Culotta complained. "Gator Trace just won't be the same here with no gators."

Big Mike De Luca slammed his new Calloway titanium driver into his golf bag. "Let's pick up the pace," he grumbled.

...56

JOSEPH "BATS" BATTAGLIA GRIPPED HIS CANE and limped into the orthopedic surgeon's office in Vero Beach. Battaglia was dressed casually but neatly in a sport shirt. His face was the pleasant face of an old man, worn with lines and deep shadows under the eyes, all of which were the result more of the life he had led than of the accumulated years.

He stole a glance at his new thousand-dollar Tag Heuer Classic watch: 1:45 P.M. When Battaglia approached the counter, a frosted glass panel slid open. The grim-faced, dark-haired receptionist looked at him over her glasses with obvious disinterest. "Photo ID and insurance. Then sign the register and take a seat. Doctor is running late."

Fifty elderly people sat crowded in the waiting room, struggling with multi-paged medical forms, doing crossword puzzles, reading two-year-old *Golf Digest* magazines, or just staring up at the ceiling with resigned expressions and tight lips, arms folded on their chests.

One hour and a half later, Bats Battaglia hobbled up to the closed glass panel. With a sharp noise he slapped his solid oak cane hard against the edge of the counter. The panel opened instantly. Her mouth agape, the receptionist stared wide-eyed. Battaglia pointed at his new watch. "My appointment was for 2 o'clock. Now can we cut the crap?"

"Yes, sir," she mumbled in fear and bewilderment. "I'll get the doctor right away."

The waiting room burst into spontaneous applause.

ON LAKE OKEECHOBEE at sunrise, Salvatore Scarlotti unhitched his new twenty-one foot, Nitro fiberglass bass fishing boat from his Dodge Ram 1500. He loaded onboard an over-sized cooler, a six-pack of beer, a cheese sandwich in a brown paper bag, and a dozen fragmentation hand grenades.

Starting up his Mercury 225 motor, Scarlotti headed out over the misty lake towards Cochran's Pass. A little later, three hollow-sounding explosions pierced the stillness of the Lake Okee-chobee morning. Underwater shock waves produced by the ex-ploding grenades stunned the fish, causing their bladders to rup-ture. Most of the fish sank to the lake floor, but some of the dead bass floated to the surface, to be scooped up in Scarlotti's net and dumped into his cooler.

He felt a little weary by the time the cooler was stuffed full. Scarlotti checked his watch: 9 A.M. Time to go. As he pulled up the sea anchor, two fishermen drifted by using a trolling motor to keep their boat lined up and straight. One of them shouted over the water, "Catching anything?"

"So so," he replied without enthusiasm.

"The wind's right for jigs and minnows," the fisherman re-marked, "but no luck. They must be blasting at the Taylor Creek reservoir construction site. It's spooking the fish."

"We can't even catch a cold," the other fisherman said.

Crazy Sal Scarlotti shrugged. "That's why they call it *fish-ing*, not *catching*." He opened a can of beer and piloted his new Nitro bass fishing boat back towards shore.

...58

ROSALIE WOLFFE'S SISTER Gertrude owned a condominium apartment in Hunter's Run, an upscale residential community located in Boynton Beach, in the heart of Palm Beach County. Rosalie enjoyed her divorced sister's company and also the fact that Gertrude lived close by trendy Atlantic Avenue, fifteen minutes from Boca Raton and twenty minutes from the Palm Beach Garden Mall.

"Jack Solomon was very taken with you in the yoga class, Rosie," her sister confided. "You should go out with him."

"Marcus has only been dead a month."

"According to the papers, the man was connected to the Mafia and drug dealers. Didn't you ever suspect anything?"

"Marcus was a quiet man. He talked in his sleep, in foreign languages. But—"

"All men are scum," Gertrude interrupted. "My Joel ran off with his blonde *shiksa* stockbroker from Merrill Lynch." She paused to take in a breath. "We're not getting any younger, Rosie. Soon the arthritis—then the Depends. You always liked to dance and have fun. Go out, meet somebody."

Rosalie kept silent.

"And from what I hear, Jack Solomon is well fixed financially—and otherwise."

Rosalie blushed. "I'm still in mourning."

"Well then, honey, let's go up to the Gardens Mall. Victoria's Secret has just what you're looking for: one hundred percent silk bikini panties on sale—and in *black*."

"I guess it wouldn't hurt to look," Rosalie Wolffe replied with a tight smile.

...59

THE SUNRISE THEATRE in Fort Pierce buzzed with activity. Mayor Willie Westlake had skillfully arranged for students to be bussed in to fill the balcony. City employees, given the afternoon off, jammed the orchestra section. In the first row sat specially invited guests.

"Is Rosalie here?" Rizzo asked Joe De Luca in a hushed voice.

"No. She's in Boynton Beach with her sister."

"The papers said Rosie's husband was a *Capo*."

De Luca shrugged. "Yeah. And I'm George Clooney."

As the white-shirted members of the Avenue D Boy's Choir finished their first selection, Mayor Westlake strode to the lectern with a practiced smile, clapping his hands. The tall, well-built Afro-American man with a mop of white hair wore a dark suit, a white shirt and a black tie. "That's a truly *amazing* version of 'Amazing Grace,' " Westlake quipped.

A small ripple of laughter came from the audience

"Avenue D in Fort Pierce," Westlake said in a more serious voice, "is known for a lot of things, most of them not very positive. The Boys' Choir was purposely named after this street to show support for our friends and neighbors who are working hard to overcome a widespread negative image."

Whistles came from the balcony.

"I would like to acknowledge the presence of the media today. As many of you know, the nation's mayors will be holding their national leadership meeting in Jacksonville to develop an agenda to deal with budgetary considerations in these difficult economic times." He paused for effect. "I am honored to be the keynote speaker at that important event."

The city employees applauded—as scripted.

"As I announced three months ago, with the recession affecting Fort Pierce's budget at every level, expenses would be trimmed. We were not going to have deficit spending, and we're not going to borrow from future generations, so we made do with fewer police officers. I initiated a 'Partners on Patrol' program utilizing outsourced volunteers, and I am pleased to report the results: Overall crime in Fort Pierce is down 19 percent and violent crime for the comparable period is down 38 percent."

The audience applauded again.

Westlake continued. "According to the latest police reports, the majority of the crime reduction has occurred in the Lincoln Park neighborhoods, which in the past had seen violent crime rates as high as 10 times the national average."

The boys' choir sang "Nearer, My God, to Thee."

Mayor Westlake returned on stage clapping. "Aren't they wonderful?" He continued, "As a direct result of our efforts to reduce the influence of gangs in the Lincoln Park area, I am also proud to announce that in the last few months, school attendance has increased, we have added a girl's choir to the Avenue D family, and the 'Learn to Read' mentoring program has reported an increase of applicants."

More applause.

"At this time," Westlake continued, "I wish to pay tribute to special volunteers who assisted the police in achieving these outstanding reductions in crime statistics. Their selflessness and community spirit bring to mind one of my favorite quotations: '*I do get paid for my volunteer work. I just don't get paid money.*' "

"You cheap bastard," Battaglia mumbled audibly.

"When I call their names, I would ask each of the following individuals to rise. Please hold your applause until they are all standing. Mr. Michael De Luca. Mr. Salvadore Scarlotti. Mr. Edward Rizzo. And, last but not least, Mr. Joseph Battaglia. Let's give them a sincere Fort Pierce round of applause."

The audience rose as one to give a standing ovation to the four members of the Orange Blossom Security Agency.

...60

TWO WEEKS LATER, FRANK FERNANDEZ listened to the steeple clock on St. Andrew's Church strike the hour of 5 o'clock in a melodious chime. "Except for the hurricanes, Mr. Fernandez, October in Fort Pierce is my favorite month," sprightly real estate agent Remy Cortland explained. He studied her face, her full bosom, her large dark eyes, frosted hair and sensual smile. Remy was in her forties, he figured.

"You will love Fort Pierce. We have the Sunrise Theatre and the A.E. Backus Museum. And this building, 505 South 2nd Street, is a short walk to the Indian River Lagoon waterfront."

The real estate agent added, "Having your Orange Blossom Security Agency located at this address will offer your clients added confidence, knowing that the FBI offices are on the third floor and Homeland Security leases the entire first floor."

"Thank you, Remy. I haven't made a final decision to move or to buy the company. Bank loans are hard to come by. I will need a little time to sort it all out."

She smiled and moved closer as if she wanted to straighten out his tie. "Here is my card. I'm single and a great cook. If you would like to come over for something nourishing, give me a call."

Fernandez felt aroused watching the woman's statuesque figure in high heels clack down the parking lot to her car. His necktie was missing, but he was still dressed in a white shirt and wrinkled dark blue suit. He vaguely noticed the palm tree fronds ruffling in the breeze.

The ringing of his iPhone broke the silence. He looked at the screen and then pressed a finger against his free ear.

"Martin? What's up?"

"Your test results are back."

"Tell me."

"The films showed an interarticular invasion of the bullet fragments. Your blood tests established that you have microctic anemia with very high blood lead levels."

"Give it to me in plain English."

"Exposed adults should have blood lead levels below 40 micrograms. Yours is greater than 90. I spoke to the leading specialist in the field of lead poisoning, Redonda Marcus from Mayo Clinic. She recommends that you start on chelation therapy immediately."

Fernandez swallowed, but he had no saliva.

"There is always a risk associated with chelation therapy. People have died due to cardiac arrest caused by hypocalcemia." Fernandez heard his brother inhale sharply. "In addition, there is an outside chance that therapy could result in kidney failure—which would require dialysis—"

Before his brother could finish, Fernandez broke in. "Thank you, Martin. Be well. I love you." He disconnected the call, picked up his black attaché case and ambled down Second Street, passing the Sunrise Theatre, then took a right to the river.

The wind blowing in from the south felt strong but warm. Fernandez sat down on a wrought iron bench, gazing fixedly at the dark water of the Indian River. Overhead a pair of herons glided across the darkening sky. A young couple exited the library walking arm-in-arm towards the marina. He had a pang of loneliness. Latisha crossed his mind: that dark-skinned, exasperating young beauty with the exquisitely sculpted face and exciting sexual appetites.

Fernandez felt uncomfortable about their parting, the critical tone of his voice, his stomping off. He wanted to call and make up for it by saying something kind. But he couldn't think of anything. Impulsively, he took out his iPhone and tapped *Favorites*.

"Frank. Is it you? I am just so pleased that you called."

"Latisha, I owe you an apology for my boorish behavior."

"No. No. Frank," she jumped in. "It was all my fault. I have been thinking of you so much lately." She paused. "I wanted to come down to Florida to see you."

Fernandez swallowed and forced himself to breathe deeply. "That would be very special for me, Latisha. We could—"

She interrupted again. "Daddy is raising funds to run in the Florida primary, and just over twenty percent of Florida's residents are Hispanic or of Latin descent. So, Daddy and I were thinking that you might be willing to join our campaign and handle the Latino voters. You speak their language, and they will respect the fact that you were in the FBI, and Daddy says—"

"Good talking to you." Fernandez terminated the call with a thumb. The wind ruffled his hair and shook the foliage on the tall palm trees over his head.

Memorial Service for Former FBI Director

NEW YORK TIMES—Former FBI Director William Glenner died from a gunshot wound suffered during a suspected robbery at his retirement home in Charlotte Amalie East in the U. S. Virgin Islands. A memorial service will be held in Washington on Sunday. The President will give the eulogy for the popular 54-year-old former FBI director.

Louisiana Congressman Clarence Du Burns told the *Times*, "Our republic has been well served by men of dedication and integrity like William Glenner. His wise counsel will be sorely missed by all of us in Congress—regardless of political party."

The head of the U.S. Virgin Islands Police Department, Henry Jennings, reported that every effort is being undertaken to find Glenner's killer. Jennings told CNN that the Charlotte Amalie East medical examiner reported finding a small caliber bullet hole in the upper center of the victim's forehead. The ME reported that it was the kind of shot that bled very little, caused instantaneous death and looked like the man had three eyes.

USING HIS iPHONE, Fernandez finished reading the *New York Times* article. He took a breath and then squeezed his eyes shut for a second. He sat on the bench with his head in his hands. A large pouched brown pelican unfolded its wings and launched clumsily into the air. Spotting a fish, the carnivore plunge-dived, dropping like a stone into the river. The ex-agent stared into the steel-gray water, preparing for what had to be done.

Fernandez picked up his attaché case and walked slowly north towards the high bridge crossing over the Indian River, stopping along the way to pick up large stones that he placed carefully into his jacket pockets.

At the top of the bridge, Frank Fernandez paused and opened his attaché case for the last time. He checked to see if the used American Airline tickets to the Virgin Islands were inside, along with his forged passport and the black-finished Compact Glock 357. To these items he added the stones collected en route. He locked the case and dropped it over the bridge, where it sank into the deepest part of the Indian River. The wind gusted up. There was still a hint of pink in the darkening sky.

CPSIA information can be obtained at www.ICGtesting.com
Printed in the USA
LVOW112356230312

274479LV00001B/2/P

9 780983 780366